Curiosities is a thrice annual publication of speculative short fiction in the retropunk subgenres.

We've saved our darkest stories for the darkest months of the year. In this volume you will meet clockwork children, demonic doppelgangers, doomed gunslingers, skeletal servitors, infected flappers, haunted roadhouses, and maybe glimpse at Old Scratch himself.

Come, sit close to the fire and explore our winter exhibits of horror and dread.

WINTER HORROR AND

NUMBER FIVE

CURIOSITIES

DREAD

STORIES BY ✣ IRENE PUNTI ✣ SANTIAGO EXIMENO
MADELEINE SHANN ✣ GEORGE EDWARDS MURRAY
GARY BULLER ✣ SAMANTHA LEE ✣ MARIA HASKINS
ANDREA MARTINEZ CORBIN ✣ SHELIAH LINDSEY
ALEXANDER STANMYER ✣ BESTON BARNETT

Curiosities #5 Winter 2019.
©2019 by Kevin Frost

"All She Needs" ©2018 by Madeleine Swann.
"Barbed Wire Fence" ©2016 by Santiago Eximeno. Translated from Spanish by Alicia L. Alonso.
"The Cheshire's Grin" ©2018 by Irene Punti.
"Elmore Banks Was a Bad Man and His Gun Had a Name and Her Name Was Celia"©2018 by Alexander Stanmyer.
"Fixable"©2017 by Sheliah Lindsey.
"Lady With a Thousand Teeth" ©2017 by George Edwards Murray.
"A Light in the Darkness" ©2018 by Gary Buller.
"The One in the Night-Storm Dress" ©2018 by Andrea Martinez Corbin.
"Scent"©2016 by Maria Haskins, first appeared in *Flash Fiction Online* September 2016.
"Take Five" ©1977 by Samantha Lee, first appeared in print in *Fantasy Tales* Vol. 8 No.15 Winter 1985.
"The Unusual Commission" ©2018 by Beston Barnett.

Cover art: "Little Tophet" ©2018 by Toe Keen.
Flatware clip art via The Old Design Shop.
Other clip art via Shutterstock.

ISBN-13: 978-1-948396-08-0 (Print on Demand)
ISBN-13: 978-1-948396-09-7 (EPUB)

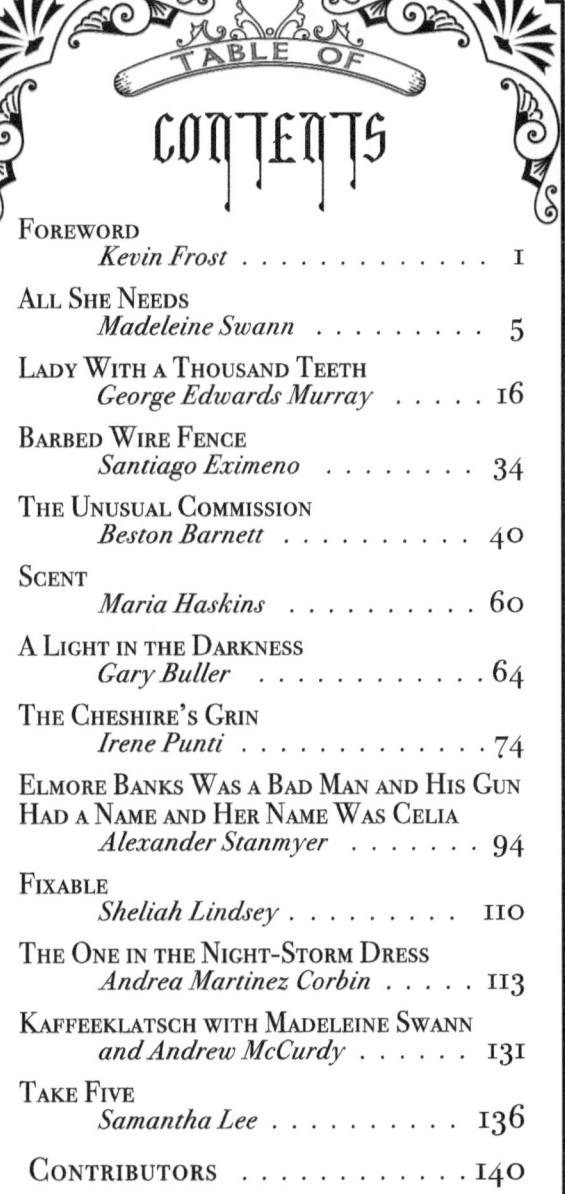

CONTENTS

It's been a cold winter here on the mesa. The kind of cold that gets into your bones and makes the long muscles of your legs tight like so many strands of meat jerky. Those of us who sleep solo find it better to break out the expedition weight sleeping bag rather than get under the covers and try to warm the whole bed alone, and the dogs come to rouse me in the night, hoping I will understand that the stove needs more wood. In other words, it's a good season for horror stories.

The feedback on the first issue of Curiosities told me that mixing the horror stories in with the others might not have been the best idea. Our slush pile self-organizes into broad themes, so since then, we've been sorting the stories into their potential issues as the contracts are signed, rather than assigning them to the next issue on the calendar. My own preference for anthologies is the box of chocolates approach, rather than the topical deep dive, but that does not appear to be as popular. I think this is a good compromise.

Most of the selections on this round caused a lot of discussion with the reading crew. I don't remember any of these stories being unanimous picks. Horror is a strange beast that way, as everyone has their own peculiar limits for what is pleasantly creepy and what has just gone too far. These stories that made us argue to keep our favorites on the table, which made us all think harder about what we were doing. As we are still a young market, that was not a bad thing.

Madeleine Swann's 1920s London flapper story has such a strong voice that it has proven difficult to find a narrator for. Between her flamboyant wardrobe and *Silent Motorist* noting her as one of "10 Weird Writers to Save Us All in 2018," I wanted to know more, so I sent Andrew off to interview her. Also in the jazz era is Samantha Lee's reprint which first appeared on a late night radio show in the 1970s. It has been reprinted several times, but she wanted it to bring it back to its roots, as an audio piece.

There are two war pieces here which felt better to save for the horror issue: Santiago Eximeno's weird trench warfare piece, one of the few translations we have ever received, and George Edwards Murray's brooding story about war and innocence, which was Steadman's favorite. Beston Barnett sent a colorfully textured period piece reminiscent of those old AIP films I loved as kid, back when Jack Nicholson played the young romantic lead. It is told by a Jewish voice during the Spanish Inquisition. Mr Beston happily informed me that he received his acceptance letter while he was in the middle of a class critique at Clarion.

Maria Haskins' dark fantasy tale was so disturbing that the narrator stopped dead in her tracks at the reveal. I will be adding that outtake to her episode when it airs. It pairs nicely with Sheliah Lindsey's steampunk flash piece. Would that double be too dark for Mother's Day? Let me know.

Gary Buller, one of our 'frequent flyers' since his first sale with us in 2016, finally figured out how to crack the algorithm with a classic ghost story inspired by an old EC comic. We all agreed that our reactions to Andrea Martinez Corbin's coming-of-age piece were 'complicated' but its compelling prose won the day. As a post-apocalypse fan, Irene Punti's worldbuilding won me easily, with its strange blend of ancient Rome, genetic engineering, and her snarky nod to reenactor culture.

And finally, we must talk about Alexander Stanmyer's Lovecraftian western. When Mr Stanmyer's very long title appeared in my inbox, I thought to myself, please let it be good. It did not disappoint, but it did go beyond what we've allowed for previously with regards to cussing. When we buy a story which contains swearing, I often ask the author for a seperate 'audio edit' to make it less harsh to the ear. Maybe because I was a sailor who had to unlearn my nautical manners before I could be allowed to stand at the head of a classroom, or maybe I think you might be listening to the podcast while you have the kids in the car with you. If you're going to drop the f-bomb, make it a fifty dollar word, not cheaply scattered pocket change, and God forbid you use it as punctuation. Weird westerns are the grittiest of the steam era* stories, so I felt Mr Stanmyer's use of profanity was well justified and let it pass. And like Madeleine Swann's piece, it has proven difficult to place with with a narrator.

This issue nearly empties out our print backlog so we will be having another reading session in April. The next two themes are (tenitavely) Steampunk and World War 2. There is also a growing column which we can't quite pin a name on, for quirky stories that defy categorization. Our guilty pleasures, if you will.

The audio backlog is ever growing. There are a good number in the production queue that have made it back from narration, which means I need to get my seat in the chair and put the headphones on. Only one contract has expired so far without being recorded. I do expect more stories will slip past their expiration dates by the end of this year without making it to podcast. Alas, the time involved to produce audio creates its own limitations. Time seems to pass more quickly these days.

The dogs are nudging me again. They are not acting like they want to be let out to chase off the coyotes. I better go stoke the stove. There might be frost giants outside.

Stay warm.

Kevin Frost
Tres Piedras, New Mexico
January 2019

---

*Some of us with family roots in the 'Old West' consider the Weird West to be our own regional version of steampunk. Fight me.

All She Needs

Madeleine Swann

THE HOUSE MIGHT BE OLD and rickety, and I can't clean properly 'cause of my arthritis, but it's better this way. After a few gins young Miss wails like a spirit in chains, complaining that the place smells of fungus, but she doesn't know what she's about at those moments—it's not the walls that smell of fungus. Most of the time, though, we're happy.

She was a little 'un when I first knew about the things, in 1912 or 1911. Out in the grounds, she was, on that misty morning— underneath the heron topiary with Master Ben. He was the son of Madam's bridge partner and a proper handful if he didn't get his way. I'd watched them play cup and ball from the window where I was changing the beds. Then young Miss held her hand up to Master and his face went all queer, like. He stared at it, then yanked it towards his mouth. Of course I rushed down the back stairs and charged outside. He was suckling like a babe on her wrist and they both jumped apart when they saw me. "What are you hiding?" I said, grabbing her hand. There was an odd little lump on her skin, red and raw like a pustule. "You're a dirty boy," I said to Master and they both wailed like the clappers. I carried her in, leaving him behind, and set to wrapping a bandage. Well, blow me if it hadn't completely disappeared.

By this point the Master's mother heard his weeping and they left in a hurry, Madam following them to the motor-car apologising and making arrangements for this and that, but we both knew they'd never come back. Afterwards she was even colder to Miss if that were possible. I took the little mite's mind off it though; she followed me around sweet as anything, sometimes even helping me with the dusting and sweeping—only when Madam wasn't around of course. The rest of the time she'd play tiddlywinks or just look up at me with those big blue eyes as if to tell me she wished I was her mother.

After the war, Madam and Sir were merry again and I finally became Head Housekeeper. When Miss was 17 she went to stay in London with relatives. I was heartbroken though it wouldn't do to show it, hugging her when she kissed my cheek. I wrote a few times but got nothing back. I didn't take it personal, that Aunt and Uncle of hers were forever rushing her about and I was busy enough keeping the scullery maid from nattering.

Two and a half years later whispers went round the staff that she was coming back. The maids had plenty of ideas why but soon learned to keep quiet when I was around. Her Aunt and Uncle ran off as soon as dropping her at the door, and no wonder if they allowed her to go about how she was, her face caked with make-up and lashes big spidery things. The collar was upturned on her black mink coat and her hair—my goodness! There was nothing left, just a short blonde hat. She seemed to have grown a foot taller—and a darn sight skinnier.

Sir and Madam's faces were dark as chimney sweeps. The maids took her suitcase and she smiled when she saw me. "You look like one of them moving picture stars," I said, and she did. They were so different to my day, when we argued over whose turn it was to look through the peep-hole machine on Brighton Pier to see a flickering lady dance.

"Oh, thank you," she said, "It's terribly chic, isn't it? Look here," she leaned in, "couldn't spare a ciggy, could you? I'm simply gasping."

"That's quite enough of that," her father handed her coat to the maid and ushered her up the grand stairs, "it won't do." Miss' black dress was something I'd wear in bed instead of in public. That evening I waited until Madam and Sir were safely in the drawing room before sneaking up to her.

"Oh, heavens," she exclaimed too loudly, "You really are a brick, Gladys." She lit up with an exaggerated sigh, posing against the wall like some starlet. "They have such parties in London." She giggled, "Mavis flashed a police officer and spent the night in a cell. It was rather hilarious," she laughed as if she could convince me it were anything other than scandalous.

"Sounds like you had a lovely time," I straightened the straps of her flimsy outfit, "but it's nice to be home, isn't it?" She rolled her eyes.

"They don't want me here," she jabbed a finger. I'd never seen her look so ugly. "I'll be damned if I have to listen to mummy and daddy tell me I've ruined myself again. I can't wait to get back to London. Harold and the others will be missing me awfully."

"Well," I patted her head, "it'll all come out in the wash." When I shut the door behind me I heard sobbing. She just needs a good night's sleep, I told myself, and went back to my quarters.

The next morning she was sprawled over the landing,

that skinny body of hers spilling from her peach dressing gown. Her knuckles were white as she gripped the telephone earpiece and the wire had upturned the little table. Beside her was a small, empty bottle of gin. Little so-and-so must have snuck it in. She was sobbing like she'd vomit her gizzards. "Albert," she said, "I need you, I'm going off my head. I'm so frightfully alone. Where's Harold?" I tidied up best I could, shushing her and carrying her back to her room. "I was talking," she slurred, breathing fumes you could set a match to. "It was important."

"Not as important as hiding you from your poor parents," I said, tucking her into bed. I hid the soda siphon in the cupboard and the bottle in my apron, leaving her snoring. I told Madam and Sir she'd caught a fever and they thought no more of it.

That night a young man in spats and a dinner jacket arrived at the door looking less than happy, "I've come to see Emily."

Sir heard his voice and came charging from the smoking room still in his jacket. "Now look here, what you want with my daughter?"

"I say," the young man took a step back, "steady on, she rang me this morning. I'm nothing but a friend, old chap."

"Don't you 'old chap' me," said Sir, but I could tell he was relenting. "She's been frightfully poorly, perhaps a visit would do her good. Gladys, could you escort this gentleman to Emily and stay in case they need anything?"

"Very good sir," I curtseyed. The staff should have known not to ask what happened in the room afterwards but by golly they still tried.

"Oh, Albert," Miss leaped from her bed and wound up the gramophone to play that racket youngsters listen to. "You came! Now we can have a party. Gladys, you'll join us, won't you?" She flung her limbs and laughed like a mad thing.

Albert looked about the room as if he'd lost something, "Emily, dear, I was rather under the impression that this was an emergency."

"Oh, don't be a bore."

"Honestly," the young man looked down at his feet, as if he couldn't bear to see her. His jaw wiggled as he ground his teeth. "I love you dearly, Emily, but you're an absolute cope. It's dreadfully tiresome I tell you. I was about to visit my father this evening, I've not seen the old man for weeks."

"I'm sorry," Miss' shoulders slumped, "Harold doesn't wish to see me anymore, does he?"

Albert rubbed his temples. "I'm sorry, old bean. I know things have been difficult since the others... couldn't see you anymore. I want to help but it's too much."

He turned to leave and the effect on Miss was like earth crumbling beneath a flower. She fell to her knees, "why don't they like me anymore? How can they be so beastly?" Albert sighed heavily.

"Oh, hell, you know why. You frightened them. They... frightened themselves."

"I only wished for them to like me," Miss was really sobbing now, "it just happens." I wanted Albert to leave so he'd stop hurting her with nasty words. I took the situation into my own hands, hurrying to her side and rubbing her shoulder. "There, there," I said, turning my back against him. She peeked over my shoulder and called his name but I heard the door shut. She was safe now.

The next few weeks were wonderful. She followed me about like a sweet little toddler, knitting a mauve scarf and smiling when I breezed through. Even Jonathan, the new young gardener, commented and he never noticed anything important. Spring had arrived and I saw to it that the ash in the hearths was replaced with vases of fresh smelling flowers. Miss would sigh and stare out the window, but I knew she was pining for something that could never be.

One morning in mid May though, it all changed again. She had gone to the shops alone, taking only the driver and promising to return before Sir and Madam found out. In she came, full of smiles like the first day back from London and covered once more in her clown's costume. She embraced me and I caught a whiff of something musty, moulding. I hoped it was just a poor choice of perfume. "I've made a wonderful new friend," she said, launching herself into the armchair. "We got on so famously it was as if we'd met years ago."

"Is that so?" I kept my voice even. "How lovely."

"Oh yes," she gushed, "she's the daughter of that American family who moved into the big house across the green. She has the most marvellous thick, dark hair, quite unlike mine, but she reminded me of myself in a fashion. We both find this place so very tedious; it would be criminal not to invite her for tea, don't you think?"

"Well, I..."

"I shall mention it to papa." She was gone before I could count my thoughts.

The next week there she was, on our doorstep, everything I suspected her to be. I don't care how much new money her family have, Americans are uncouth and uncivilised. She had on one of those ridiculous flower pot hats that were the fashion and a long fur scarf. Her respectable tea gown underneath didn't fool me. "Gosh," she squealed when Miss appeared at the top of the stairs, "don't you look the cat's meow?" Indeed she did in her lilac dress, but I didn't see that it was any of that little tramp's business.

"Oh, do go on," Miss laughed and the pair disappeared upstairs. I could hear everything that was said through the door though, the little minxes.

"I'd sure like to spend a night on the town with him!"

"He is simply divine." Then they flounced out, brazen as could be, and disappeared into the night to do goodness knows what.

I'd hoped it was the last I'd see of the American, that Sir and Madam would disapprove as heartily as I, but they not only put up with this interloper, they actively encouraged it. "Nice to see her so jolly," said Sir, and Madam did the polite thing and agreed with her husband. Miss herself was acting like a woman smitten.

"She's the bee's knees," she'd gush. They said they went to the pictures but I knew they were drinking and meeting undesirables. They were never anything but sweet when they came back so Sir and Madam never suspected a thing. Oh, how it hurt me to curtsey to this urchin and ask if she needed refreshments.

"Golly," she would say in her grating accent, "I'm just fine." Miss would laugh and shut the door against me, as if she were ashamed to show how much I meant to her. I told myself it was natural she should show off, that she would be back soon. It all came to a head sooner than expected.

Sir and Madam were spending a night at the Purnell's out in the Fens, leaving Miss at home with her new friend. They should have known better for no sooner were they in the motorcar than that American was on the telephone to all and sundry. "Miss," I said as sternly as I could, "is this wise?"

"I say," she raised an eyebrow, "one ought to know better than to boss the Lady of the House, wouldn't you agree?"

"You're a card," said that girl. I could have slapped her but instead I made myself busy in the room, watching them make calls promising a night of music, 'booze' as they called it and heavens knows what else.

"It'll be darling, you must come" purred Miss. Once all had been summoned they squealed like a pair of pigs.

"Boy, I wish I could be all slinky class like you," pouted the American.

"Nonsense, darling," Miss searched her wardrobe and pulled out a black number I would expect her to wear down the docks waiting for sailors, "why don't you try this?" She turned to me as I pretended to dust the book case. "Gladys, I dare say your duties are finished for the evening. One mustn't be a nuisance." I left clutching my feather duster like a weapon. They would find out what a nuisance 'one' can be.

From my room I heard footsteps after footsteps, thuds and shrieks of laughter, cheers as each new person entered and all the while that gramophone cranking away. Every now and then it wound down to shouts of merry disappointment, but always it found its way on again. The maids and manservants muttered savagely from their rooms but I just smiled. It wouldn't be long now.

After a few hours of that interminable racket something changed. Softer music leaked through the ceiling and the conversation quietened. I snuck out, still in my nightdress. All the lights outside the servant's quarters were on and I went up the grand stairs, unsure if I wanted to see what was up there. I stood on the landing and listened. Lyrics poured under the door, *"birds do it, bees do it, even educated fleas do it..."* but beneath that were slurps and squishes, mumbles and moans. They couldn't be...

"Right, stand aside," boomed the voice of Sir beside me, and Madam was right behind him. Oh, why hadn't they arrived sooner? I didn't even hear them come in. He pushed the door open—silly lamb hadn't even locked it—and charged in. "What the Devil..." he staggered back. There, on the floor, were three strange young men and two women in various states of undress. That American floozy was completely starkers and all leaned over Miss' prone, naked body.

It wasn't quite the sight we had all expected to see, though, and I couldn't hear Sir and Madam's reaction on account of the creeping horrors pinching my skin. The guests sucked at protrusions sprouting from her flesh; big, dark, wet looking mushrooms—I couldn't describe them as anything else. One of the men looked up but it was as if he couldn't see. Yellow pus dribbled from his lips onto his chin which he wiped with a finger and licked, as though he couldn't bear to waste a bit of it. It was all I could do not to vomit. Miss was in plain ecstasy, moaning and groaning like a whore, her body bending this way and that, and all the while the gramophone proposing *"let's do it, let's fall in love."*

Miss saw us and squealed like a puppy in a cold room. She hopped on to her feet, the horrible things dangling like teats. Wrapping the dressing gown around her didn't help—you could see them poking through. Her friends mewled and reached for them like babes in arms until slowly they came to. The look of horror on their faces surely matched mine.

Beside me I heard an odd choking sound and a screech from Madam. At first I was angry at such a racket but when I saw Sir collapse to the floor and grab his right arm I knew there was trouble. I woke the servants and called the ambulance, making sure Sir was laid on the bed. Miss' friends slunk out like the filthy things they were and I slammed the door behind that American strumpet once and for all. Well, nearly once and for all.

The ambulance snatched him away, Madam and Miss going with them. I had to relay the story several times to the others, leaving out of course the scene in the room. Mabel, the cook, glared at me as if this was my fault, the cheeky mare. I had to call Miss' Aunt and Uncle. It's what any decent person would have done.

Sir didn't survive the night and Madam left the country after the funeral 'for her health.' At nights as I headed for bed I heard Miss making desperate calls, no doubt to those heathens. It either ended with her begging and weeping, cradling the earpiece after they'd hung up, or in an argument with the switchboard girls. "No, dear," she would fume, "you don't have to explain the rules to me again, simply try the number one last time, there's been a mistake." Then the American turned up one afternoon, bold as a brass statue, on the doorstep.

She was dressed in a long coat and skirt, a neatly wrapped present in her hands. She had at least the decency to look ashamed when she handed it to me. "Gee, uh, could you tell Emily I'm awful sorry about her father. Last time she called I was a little sharp, and..." she struggled for words so I helped her.

"Miss is very embarrassed about what happened and would prefer it if she was left alone."

The girl's eyes widened in surprise. It felt wonderful. "Well, could you tell her I'll call..."

"It's not advised. She has no wish to see you further— any of you."

"Oh." Her expression hardened and the real face came through, "Sure, I catch on, don't you worry." She stormed back to her vagabond house and I could have danced a jig. Miss appeared at the top of the stairs as I closed the door.

"Who was that, Gladys?"

"Nothing for you to worry about, Miss" I said brusquely.

"But who is that present from?"

"One of the neighbours dropped by, left it for Madam. I said I didn't know when she'd return but she insisted."

"Right." Miss looked forlorn and I wanted to tell her,

but I knew it was better in the long run. A clean break was what she needed and her father's money would see her well for the rest of her life. She had no need of that nasty place out there that made her act so uncouth and caused her such pain.

She gave up trying to contact the outside world and, one bright afternoon, we received news of Madam's death—a silly motorcar accident in Monte Carlo. Heavens knows who she was with or why they were driving so fast but it strengthened my resolve that Miss should be kept safe. One by one the other servants left and soon it was quiet bliss.

Each morning I bring Miss a cocktail else she throws a terrible fit. Her little problem has run away with itself and now she couldn't leave the house if she wanted to. I suppose the anguish must have curdled the milk inside them as she's become quite unwell. Her limbs have atrophied and mushrooms have spurted all over her body, forming a sticky crust if she stays still too long. When she wakes it's a terrible struggle to prise her out of bed but we manage.

We laugh together and play backgammon or project moving pictures in a dark room where she can forget her looks for an hour or two. I'm in charge of her alcohol intake to stop her getting silly, and I make sure she has at least a little solid food. At night she does become troublesome, weeping and wailing and sometimes smashing things, but by the morning she's my Miss again, my little Miss, and I'm all she needs.

Lady With a Thousand Teeth

George Edwards Murray

AND IN THOSE DAYS when we had such things as blue skies and moist earth—when the forests were verdant and there was such a thing as meadowland—in those days of life untampered, I found Louis standing at my doorstep, wanting to see the Lady with a Thousand Teeth for a third time.

The two times before did not count, he said, because the first time I had dawdled—I was speaking with Mrs. Bolling's daughter, Francesca, trying my hardest not to let my eyes wander down her dress—and we arrived to see the caravan folk packing up for the night. The second time so many townspeople crowded the Lady's tent we could barely see her at all. So the third time Louis came to my door he came with hungry eyes glinting, his jocund face red and mischievous and shadowy in the cracking dawn, and he all but forced me from my house, through the streets, and into the fields where the caravan dwelt.

There was nothing else for me, anyway. The university

was still shut down, awaiting the breakout of peace. And until such a time we were to sit patiently at home and wait for our numbers to be called. As if the stocky generals at the front sat in their tents, jackets gleaming with the sheen of medals and honors, saying to one another: "What we really need is a first-year student of Ancient Languages." And in the meantime I would watch from my window the machinations of my hometown, once comforting, now torpid after my taste of the metropolitan life.

So we walked to the north that morning, as the sky began to turn, Louis just ahead, his coveralls caked in layers of earth and sweat, puckish grin deforming his wiry orange beard. Myself just behind, buckled leather boots swishing through the bending sabers of grass. The air smelled of spring, still burgeoning and timid and perfect within my nose and lungs, and the hot rays of sunshine warmed my skin and hair, and all the world seemed interlocking and fitted.

These were the days in which there was such a thing as springtime.

When we reached the caravan the tents were bright and dewy with morning sun. The people of the town milled between the wagons and stands and in and out of the tents while the traveling folk, the purveyors of the entire spectacle, looked on, smiles pointed and dartlike, eyes calculating, arms wide in perpetual gestures of invitation.

Look here, look here, and see incredible feats of impossible strength!

Behold! The cabinet of freaks and malformations!

Madame Thistle's Tent of Erotic Delights! You've all heard about it! Now see it!

While I looked around and marveled, Louis did not so much as turn his head. Occasionally he would grab my shoulder and steer me with one weathered paw whenever my attention wandered.

"Hey there," I said, "How about Madame Thistle's tent?"

"You couldn't handle it."

"How about the feats of strength? That could be interesting."

Louis pointed to a cut above his eye, surrounded by a lake of bruised flesh. "What, like what the old man showed me last week? No thanks. We're not leaving without seeing the Lady."

Up ahead, all manner of townsfolk departed the Lady's tent, chatting, smiling, clapping each other on the shoulders, as if the chaos and heartbreak and desolation of war lay not just beyond their borders, and they were safe.

Looking back, I don't blame them. The mask of normality fell away only after it all was over.

We paid our fare and went inside her tent. The air buzzed with chatter and the bustle of skin on skin, people pushing and craning to look. Louis cut a path forward, his burly miner's body an ice-breaking ship, me the minnow in its wake. When we reached the front he slammed his hands upon the rickety wooden railing there, kicking up curls of sawdust, and whistled.

"Take a gander at that," he said.

I had already seen enough the second time we went, but I humored him and cast a glance in the Lady's direction, thinking of all the delights we were missing in Madame Thistle's tent. At that age I was only interested in one thing, and the lady had a cloth skirt wrapped around her waist, so I couldn't even see it. The cloth was her only garment, but her breasts were so encrusted by her affliction that they were hardly worth looking at. Between the shifting and rotating spindles and gears and coils I sometimes caught a glance of areola, or the swell of a heaving, fleshy breast, but so fleeting it could not excite me.

Louis, though. He looked her up and down. Quaffed her with his eyes. Watched as the gears embedded in her flesh moved in and out, as the cogs in her knees spun, moving her feet in mechanical rhythm. He pointed out to me her arms, outstretched, nestled within the copper plate in which she was embedded, the plate itself fastened to an upright metal framework. Like a living painting. Her limbs dripped with springs and wires and gears such that she seemed an iron moth, crucified for some unholy collection. We watched as she danced without moving, as her skin swelled and morphed and the complex machinery passed over it and under it and through it, penetrating it and becoming one with her flesh, a metamorphosing amalgam of woman and machine. When the gears in her neck spun they parted her dark lips and forced open her jaw, Louis and I stood on our toes to see down her mouth, observing the glistening, saliva-covered gears gnashing their teeth in the back of her throat. Lightning bolts of scar tissue ran from the corners of her mouth, where the skin had been stretched from the force of opening. And one of her eyes was a copper gear that twitched clockwise every second or so.

The other eye was brilliant blue. Like the sky in those days.

The townsfolk passed through and gaped, or else laughed, or gasped at her circumstance. Then they moved on, the peculiar clockwork of the Lady a forgettable distraction as they ventured outside for other beasts and wonders.

Louis made us stay for hours. Throughout the day I occasionally left, wandering among the other tents (I did not muster the courage for Madame Thistle). And when I came back, there he remained. He did not leave to eat. We lingered there until long after the others left, beyond nightfall, until the barker came inside and threw a tarp over her and squawked at us to leave. As we walked back home through the field now blue with moonlight and the stalks of grass now crisp with nocturnal coolness, the nighttime insects floating like motes of dust in beams of moonlight, Louis's eyes were aglow. He asked questions I could not answer, about whether she could be removed from her metal prism, about whether she had gears too down there under her skirt. He asked me if I thought she had a heart.

"I would be more worried about her throat," I said, trying to joke. My stomach was upset. I didn't like to look at the Lady with a Thousand Teeth. I didn't like seeing how she worked. Her complexity and beauty and uncanniness made me feel like a child. I shuddered when I thought of that one blue eye, vibrant and unblinking in turbulent metal seas.

Louis laughed. He punched me in the arm and said, "Don't make jokes outside your element. Everyone knows the women at University won't play the flute without a contract signed in triplicate."

We laughed and joked the rest of the night, and he did not mention again the Lady with a Thousand Teeth. But all during the trek back into town he kept looking over his shoulder to the darkening tents on the horizon.

———

The capitol sent an envoy each month, a chipper-faced adolescent in a glittering carriage of silver. The town would gather in the square, thousands of us packed into that space, our feet wedged in the cobblestones for hours as the mayor lectured at length about patriotism and duty. Then the envoy would step to the podium, mauve cloak whirling at his feet. He would read the news from the front, and always it would be a chain of victories, and we would applaud, and then the envoy would read aloud a list of names to join the brave men and women in the battlefield.

"So our victories may continue," he would always say.

I knew them sometimes. The people called away. It was like watching a dream of my old life—familiar faces placed in the bizarre context of war, given spears and applause. Mister Miller, the mustachioed butcher with no neck who lived just below me, and Elyse, whose last name I had forgotten, who had shifting eyes and wringing hands. She kissed me by the town fountain when we were young. Doreen, some baker's daughter, who sat on her balcony each morning and clucked her tongue in disapproval in the early mornings we went north to the caravan. Each of them hauled on stage and applauded and given armor and a spear and carried away. Every time I prayed I would hear some proclamation of final victory, or else a ceasefire, anything to reopen the university and take me away from the dull place. Sometimes I prayed he would read aloud my name, just to be free of the place.

But the war raged on, and the university remained closed, and I was apparently unfit to conscript. Louis, too, was never called. The organs of war are iron and fire, and both are borne of the mines. They needed him working. I thought of this often while perched in my window, one leg dangling above the little street that ran next to my room: that the earth would hide beneath the face of grass and trees the raw material of our undoing. As if to punish us for penetrating its surface.

I now realize that it was not punishment. The trees and grass and animals are a veneer, and fire and violence are the earth's true nature.

One day the envoy came with a parade. Military men and women in silken skirts and medals and gleaming pikes. We applauded and little children wielded swords of wood and tossed flowers plucked from the northern district. When the last cymbal crash echoed through the square and all the soldiers stood at attention, some wizened magistrate, his face as loose and sagging as his pompous robes, assumed the podium. He assured us of oncoming victory, and bade us look upon our fellow citizens, glorious soldiers all. He lectured about sacrifice and duty and all manner of empty words, and when the time came, unfurled his scroll and ran a hoary finger up and down its length and spoke the names of the men and women who would leave for combat. When he was done there was silence and I knew Louis would find me that night.

The bottle dangling from Louis's fingers glinted red and ochre in the dying light of sunset. He took swigs as we walked, not talking, letting wine dribble into his beard and down his chest. After draining the bottle he flung it into the field and belched and pointed to the tents up ahead. "Maybe they'll let us see under her skirt."

"They won't let you. We should go to Madame Thistle's tent," I said.

Louis shook his head. "Nah, let's see the Lady with a Thousand Teeth."

We walked a little farther without talking. Louis weaved back and forth, putting one quivering leg in front of the other in an approximation of a walk.

I finally said, "Maybe you should say goodbye to your father before he leaves."

"Why should I? Good riddance."

"You just seem a little upset."

"That's the stupidest thing I ever heard. I still have scars from his switch. All over." He pulled up his sleeve to show me his ravaged arm, but I did not look. I had seen it before. He rolled his sleeve back down and huffed.

"We just don't know when he'll be back." I don't know what I was trying to say. That the beast who sneered at his son's name, left welts upon his flesh, was something worthy of pity? Maybe I just didn't like seeing Louis drunk.

We were quiet for the rest of the walk. Me in cautious silence, Louis taciturn through drink and rage. All the way to the caravan his inebriated path carved serpentine waves in the delicate stalks of the field. We arrived and paid our fare and ducked inside the Lady's tent. We walked to the front and stayed there, Louis hanging onto the barrier for support, his knees trembling, his whole body rocking back and forth. Few others were there. When cast against the day's pageantry the caravan, now in its fourth month of residence, was bland and unexciting.

Louis mooned for some time before he turned to me and said, "This is how it should be for all of us." He threw a limp hand in the Lady's direction. Her head oscillated back and forth and her mouth opened and shut and opened again, wide, painfully wide, and her gears spun in and out of her skin.

"Everything makes sense when you can see its parts," Louis continued, his words slurring together. "One gear turns another and that gear winds a spring and that spring coils and uncoils and it makes her arm move. And you can see it all, and follow it back to the source, and you know what's going to happen, what's already happened, and why it all happens. And nothing doesn't make sense."

He leaned backwards, balancing on his heels, pulling at the creaking barricade. "I bet, I bet if we cracked open her skull we could see all the little gears in there and tell what she's thinking, and if we cracked open her chest we could see the gears in her heart and everything she's feeling would all make sense. You hear me, bookworm?"

I said nothing.

He looked back to her and sighed longingly. "Maybe if I touch her I'll get gears in my head."

He careened backward, and what little grip he had gave out and Louis, mighty Louis, tumbled to the ground, swearing and coughing. He pushed away my outstretched hands and attempted to stand on his own. I moved back and looked to the Lady with a Thousand Teeth.

Her gaze was fixed upon us, her flesh eye wide open and dazzling and hungry, her copper eye spinning. Struck across her hybrid face was carved a toothy smile, crescent-like and stretching from one ear to the other. Her bodily gears moved slowly and made no noise, and neither Louis nor I breathed, as together the three of us shared those minutes of mutual malfunction, immobile and intertwined.

And then Louis laughed. "She knows what I mean. Don't you?" He blew her a kiss as I pulled him to the exit.

We stumbled into moonlight and open air. As we walked through the scattering of tents and stands, Louis erupted into drunken song, I looked back and saw through the barely-parted canvas the gleaming eye of the Lady with a Thousand Teeth, thirstily gleaming at me, her dead smile growing all the wider.

After that Louis would show up nearly every morning he was free of the mines, or in the evening following his shift, and he would beg me to see the Lady with him just one more time. I always refused. Too harsh, still, remained the memory of her cycloptic gaze. The rows of teeth more pointed and menacing with each remembrance. It made me sick to think of her. No matter how Louis raved about her transparency and truth, she remained inscrutable to me. She who was an anomaly among the anomalous. Unplaced and unwelcome. Alien. She who mortified the soul with each clack of her ironflesh neck. I refused again and again, and soon Louis came by infrequently, and in the months that followed he stopped haunting my doorstop altogether.

I had hoarded all the paper I could when rumors spread of a ration. I used every sheet I had. I wrote to my professors, asked them if they knew when school would reopen, said that I wanted to enroll a friend as quickly as I could, that I would pay for his tuition if they would just take him. The post had stopped, so I asked a local birdkeeper for use of his trained pigeons. He stopped letting me use them when one came back holding a severed finger. My professors never wrote back.

All the while the trees grew bright and died and then grew bright again. I tried in vain to distract myself. The few books I had from school were not so entertaining upon the third, fourth, fifth readings. I went for walks through town and the forest. I avoided the fields, where still lay the billowing mountains of the caravan. Travel between towns became restricted, so it could not leave. Even if it could, I felt it would not. Not while the Lady had one victim.

The war crept from the east. Sometimes when I walked and my ear was attuned with the wind I would hear, so faint and so low but still there, a sound like mighty thunderclaps, weighted with gloom. Mostly at night. I knew what it was, what it heralded. For the sake of my neighbors I did not speak of it.

Soon there hung above the town floating warships, crawling in a west-to-east convoy toward the raucous thunder on the horizon. A line of dots bound for sunrise. The tattered canvas of their ovoid hulls was stained and ripped and bore the faded colors of our homeland. Their names painted on their sides in chipping paint, once-fearsome monikers now impotent with time and use. Throughout the day they trickled across the sky in single file, and at fall of night they became drifting blotches of starlessness. No one talked about them. We traded. We laughed. We sang. But we didn't speak of the line of machinery overhead.

The monthly ceremony continued. More and more called to the draft. No more pageantry. No more pomp. A simple list of names read aloud by aging youth. The weathered souls who stepped forward were quickly shoved aside and carted into darkness.

Louis was always at these gatherings. Each time the flesh of his face clung ever more to his skull, and the dirt along his arms and legs became darker and coarser. I wanted to reach out and touch him, confirm the bedraggled corpse in the crowd was Louis, my friend Louis, and not some rocking, shambling thing which wore his skin.

At one gathering, near the end of things, when the sky stayed red in daytime, Miss Florence, who now lived in Mister Miller's old room, caught me staring at the Louis-thing. She said to me, "They are working the miners very hard, you see."

"Yes, I've heard," I said, not taking my eyes from the wasting beast beyond. Everyone in town knew Louis had not reported to the mines in months. If his father was home he would have beaten Louis for laziness or insubordination or any half-formed transgression to explain the sorry state of his offspring. Or maybe he would have simply looked his son up and down and not bothered.

Of course it was Her. In red dawn and coral twilight and all time and color between he stumbled through the streets, bottle to his lips, dragging himself northward. I never went out and stopped him. None of us did. No-one brought him into a room, gave him a warm blanket and tea and a friendly ear. Maybe, at the time, it seemed as if that staggering, incoherent mess northward was some small part in a large machine, as unknowable and distant as the warships which had become our clouds. We all were cogs in that machine. Happy and spinning until our doomsday.

And my part: the switch too cowardly to disengage it.

I think that is why Louis continued to attend the ceremony where they culled us for the draft. For hope that someone would switch him off, take him by force to the front, where he might be killed alongside our neighbors, and never again revel in the presence of the clockwork succubus. But she would not so easily relinquish her favorite cog.

On this, the last night, the sky was violet, as was the orchid globe of the moon, and there was not birdsong, nor insect chatter nor rustle of leaves, and all the world seemed to hold its breath, and Louis was standing at my door. Twisted smirk splitting his threadbare beard, hands clutching an opaque bottle, his skeletal body leaning against the frame.

"Long time, friend," he said, and bared what remained of his teeth.

"I know."

"I don't see you at the caravan." He belched and looked at me and raised one eyebrow, as if he were expecting a confession.

"I don't like going down there."

He scoffed. "Nothing down there's going to hurt you. Not like out here." He took a swig from his bottle and teetered back and forth. Patches of scalp glowed through his once-lush red hair. Knobby elbows bulged beneath his skin like tumors. His eyes sat so far back into his skull they were little more than glistening shadows. He looked like a man half-formed, begun by some creator then abandoned halfway through.

When I did not respond he waved a hand at me and said, "Come with me tonight, old friend. I want to have some fun."

"There's a curfew."

"Says who?"

"I don't know. There's just a curfew."

"Oh, I see. *They* say." He snorted and took another drink. The bottle made a popping sound as he pulled it from his mouth. He wiped his lips on his sleeve and pointed at me. "They say I have to dig for coal and ore. But I can't really see my part in all that. So here I am." He spread his arms wide and smiled and stepped into the street and became awash with violet light, and I saw for the first time he had his bag of tools slung over his shoulder.

That night the fields came alive in the altered moonlight, just as the clouds above churned and toiled in amethyst waves, save for the drifting shadows of airships. A hot wind blew, sulfuric, and there were times I opened my mouth to yawn or cough and tasted blood in the air. From the horizon came the thump thump thump of war drawing ever-closer.

Louis did not speak until after we jumped the fence and crawled beneath the folds of the tent. The top was open and the moon blazed overhead, vibrant and luminous, and as we walked to the middle of the tent we swam in the light of an unquiet sky, and though the envoys and clerics foretold otherwise, I knew that night we trod in a dying land.

The tent seemed larger without the curious townsfolk shuffling through it. The edges of were mired in darkness, but in the center, trapped in a beam of violet moonlight, stood the cloth-gird frame of the Lady with a Thousand Teeth. She ticked and tocked faintly from beneath her canvas blanket. Louis swaggered forward, dropping his empty bottle, and with a shaky hand sent the sheet cascading into the dust.

She was asleep. Or at least her eyes were. The rest of her clicked and spun, gently, both above and below her skin. Her fingers, splayed at the ends of her outstretched arms, slowly furled and unfurled in time with the machinations of her innards. Her mouth stayed closed.

Louis's laughter echoed throughout the place. I did not ask him what he found so funny. Nothing was funny anymore. Not really.

He clasped her hand, letting her fingers curl around his. She did not wake.

"You think she knows what's going on?" he said.

"She probably doesn't even have feeling in her fingers," I said. "Just forget her, Louis."

"That's not what I meant." He stroked her hair, taking care not to accidentally thread it through her machinery. "Do you think she knows about everything? About the war and the envoys and the draft and the mines? Do you think she even knows what war is? Or hate? Or death? Do you think she knows she's in a country, someplace on one side of an imaginary line?"

I said nothing.

After a while Louis said, "I think so, too," not taking his eyes from her. He ran an emaciated finger around her cheek bones, brushing it against her sleeping eyes. He put a hand on either side of her head and held them there, and said, "I come here every day. They let me in for free—the caravan folk—because they know. They see how she looks to me and me to her and they see two people who understand. And when she sweeps her gaze across the room she pauses upon me, because she can hear the gears in my heart, and she knows they are in sync with hers."

He ran fingers deep through her hair and turned to me. His eyes were wide and deep and twinkled dully in the shafts of moonlight. In that moment I saw nothing of the friend I once knew, of the friend who saw me off to university with playful teasing and jest, who taught me about women and wine. Louis was right: he had gears in his heart. But they were not placed by the Lady with a Thousand Teeth. They were always there. The gears that produced the false romance of The Simple Life, of the Glory of War. The gears of a small town at the edges of a war it knew nothing about, but assumed would be decorous and sweet. The Lady with a Thousand Teeth did not place these gears; she only bade them spin.

The air became frigid. Louis chuckled as the wind whipped against the side of the tent, and the percussive rhythm of artillery grew louder, louder than ever before, like the approach of giant feet, and all the world seemed cast into violence. And at the epicenter was the sleeping Lady with a Thousand Teeth, her body quietly humming and clicking and turning.

From his bag Louis pull a wrench. "I need your help," he said, raising his voice over the howl of the wind. "Hold her steady while I undo the frame. Then I'm going to get her out of that metal plate and she and you and me are going to go somewhere far away, away from the war and university and the mines." He grinned so hard I though his jaw would break. He tapped his wrench against his palm, waiting for me to step forward.

And the cowardly switch did not turn off the machine.

When the frame was off Louis eased her onto the ground, still embedded in her plate, and then set about undoing the corona of rivets which held her there. She stayed asleep, although her cogs receded from Louis's wrench as he circled around, shrinking into her body in waves, the way one draws away from an open flame. When she was all undone and the floor was littered with discarded nuts and bolts and tabs of metal, Louis lifted the plate and heaved it to one side and there she lay in the dirt, a resting blur, her parts humming and buzzing and spinning round and round.

Outside the thunderous din continued like a heartbeat, and I felt each impact shake the ground beneath my feet.

Louis did not notice. He lay down next to her and stroked her face and kissed her unmoving lips. Deeply, fully, passionately, the little hairs of his beard caught in her movements. He ran his hands up and down her body, found the unblemished skin and caressed it, and the gears in her neck began to wind a little faster.

"Louis," I said.

He continued. I looked away. The sight nauseated me. Louis looked like he was being absorbed. When I could stand to look back I said, "Louis, let's go. Let's go and we can talk. We can even run away. But not with her. With anyone but her."

He waved me off, his lips still engaged, and I stepped back. The air was cold, so cold, and the wind howled and flung the tent this way and that, the apocalyptic drumbeat of the approaching conquest now the metronome of our demise, as the world shook and the poles of the tent buckled and swayed and little pebbles leapt into the air. Louis continued his congress with the Lady, his flesh and spirit intertwined with hers, himself unconscious, shut off. Mechanical.

Her eyes opened.

She smiled and slowly roved her eyes down, along her body, ending at her skirt. Then she looked to Louis, and then to her skirt.

In one motion he slipped his hand under.

For a moment the two stared at each other, into each other, inches apart, chest-to-chest. Then her mouth snapped open, gears in her neck spinning wildly, and she moaned, deep and menacing and unbroken, like a landslide.

Louis screamed.

He tried to pull his arm from beneath her skirt, but

could not, no matter how hard he pulled. The Lady's moan continued without a breath or pause, powerful, inhuman. From beneath her skirt came the caterwaul of a million gears whirring to life. Louis shrieked and flailed on top of her, beat at her with his free hand, but she would not let go. The whirring from below stuttered and coughed and choked, and from between her legs sprayed flumes of blood and chunks of bone and meat. Louis's screams were like an animal's. Raw. The grinding continued, as the hot remains of his hand sprayed all around the place, until he finally ripped his arm away and all that remained at its end was a spurting stump capped by a jagged knob of bone.

I staggered backward, bile on the rise, as Louis curled on the ground and whimpered and the Lady, mouth still open and emitting the ceaseless groan, stood, clanking and jerking. Louis's blood flowed down the levers and knobs and switches along her thighs, and though he tried to crawl away he was too weak, and soon she was on top of him, her gears in wild overdrive, blurry and frantic.

And Louis shouted *no*.

It was borne of neither pain nor fear. It was not an expletive. As his flesh was ground and his skin became slick with blood, and the wide-open smile of the Lady with a Thousand Teeth loomed above him, his cries were of disbelief. Short and frail. As if his Goddess had walked among his kin, and bled.

And from between her breasts there came a golden coil, twisting outward, unscrewing, and it burrowed into Louis's chest, where lay his heart. He convulsed and choked, and then he turned his head and looked at me with his aged, sad eyes one last time.

And he whispered, "They are all gears, all the way down."

I ran. Threw apart the folds of the tent and sprinted into

the darkness as the sounds of whirring gears and tearing meat and fracturing bone crescendoed, and the ground rumbled and the air roared, from the east came the sound so loud, so loud and frightening that my ears burned. The quake of explosives and cannonfire seemed to rend the earth below and all above, and I could hear the jeers of oncoming soldiers on all sides.

They are gears, all the way down.

I ran, and the fields smelled of fire, and the horizon was mottled with brilliant flares of crimson and gold.

Barbed Wire Fence

Santiago Eximeno

THE DAY I MARCHED DOWN to the front, my mother was standing next to me. Naturally she wanted to hug me, but I couldn't reciprocate. Hurt by my inevitable rejection, she watched every single one of my moves, as if by doing so she could record them into her mind forever and let her memories of me impregnate the house. My father paid no attention to me. He walked from here to there on his crutches, crossing the living room of our small house like it was the scenario of a sports event. He moved a chair here, walked around the sofa there... walking dexterously on the wooden extensions he himself had built. He fantasized with the idea of self-mutilation, amputating his leg just below the knee like some mothers did to their sons to secure for them the life of a civil servant far away from death, from weapons, from change.

He fantasized about getting a pay rise, if only he could muster up enough courage to cut just below the kneecap. My father would never understand what made me decide to go to the front. He was one of those selfish, incompetent men. He would never understand a patriot.

As I sat at the back of the lorry that would take us to the enemy lines I saw my mother crying, broken by her grief. I wanted to share her pain and cry like her, but that too was forbidden to me. So I just watched her standing in the middle of the village square. Alone. Crying for my absence as she once cried for my brother's, while the lorry drove us away to the horror of the Great War.

I shared my journey with three other soldiers, modified just like me. Across from me sat two Trenches and next to me a Bayonet, the kind with a sharp-edged weapon instead of an arm and an elusive look in their eyes. The Trenches hid their faces behind the huge rusty engine that was their mask. Steel propellers sprouted from the axis. They were nearly twenty inches wide and grazed the vehicle's ceiling, making any movement uncomfortable. They remained silent, with their hands crossed over their lap. I didn't know if they could really speak; I'd never seen any of them so close up. I remembered them from the newspaper photos of the war front that showed many of them working the land, drilling it to build the tunnels that would shelter us from the enemy. Here, close up, their faces disappeared into a dark urine-infested hole, a pit that made it impossible to discern one single human feature that might have survived the modification.

"Fag?" asked the Bayonet, and I said no, because I thought he was offering one.

He was actually asking me for a smoke, and my negative gesture made him uncomfortable. He lowered his eyes and, with his unarmed hand, fumbled inside imaginary pockets of his uniform, to no avail. The roar of the lorry's engine kept me awake, but all I wanted to do was shut my eyes and get to wherever I needed to be. To fight the enemy. To win a war that wasn't mine. To die, like my brother. Eventually, the day's tension had the better of me. Eventually, I let sleep win.

And I dreamt.

I dreamt of German soldiers, their faces covered by gas masks sprouting tubes that went inside their torsos. I dreamt of armoured cars with human faces, of Zeppelin airships driven by faceless men bombarding our small villages. And I dreamt of my father dragging his mutilated body through the village square while my brother, tethered to the ruins of the biplane that had become an unbreakable part of his body, roared with laughter and cried tears of blood.

I woke up startled and sweating, and looked out the lorry's window to feel the breeze on my face. And then I saw them, up there. So close and yet so far away. So majestic. Biplanes. Men joined to linen-covered platforms through steel wires flew over the battlefields, first on air reconnaissance missions and then on bombing tasks. When we got off the lorry it was already dark, but a handful of them still fluttered above our heads, silhouetted by the full moon. My brother had been one of them until a German shot him down. I still remember the fragments of his modified body, broken like the wood that covered the greater part of his limbs, on the day they gave us his body.

The lorry stopped next to a small outpost, nothing but a few badly stacked sandbags and a sentry covering the entrance to the commanding area in the trench. Beyond that we could sense the front, the wasteland that separated our two small subterraneous cities, paradises for rats and abandoned souls. I raised my hand to salute the man who approached us. He was a lieutenant, most likely the same age as me.

"Welcome to the front, lads," he said. "Delighted to see you." But his eyes contradicted his words.

He stared at us with the expression of a young girl entering a fair booth with her boyfriend, dragged into the stinky darkness and terrified by the prospect of seeing a horror of nature. His pupils dilated even more when he saw me standing in front of him.

"Son, how much do you weigh?" he asked me.

I stood naked in front of him. In front of them all, actually. My skin had been modified to withstand the cold and the soles of my feet had been altered so that they would not feel the dampness of the mud we trod on. They certainly wouldn't want to lose two years' work over some damned trench feet. Thus, the alleged frailty of my body, necessary in order to correctly position it, was just that, alleged. I didn't need his compassion, nor even his affection. I needed to be allowed to be part of the front, to earn my wages.

Still, I answered respectfully. He was, after all, a lieutenant.

"Five stone, sir."

The lieutenant nodded, removed his cap and rubbed his forehead with his hand.

"Fine. Fine. We're going to spread out. Son, go with the sergeant. There's another one like you waiting with him. He'll take you to your posts. Trenches, please follow me. And you, too."

He pointed to the Bayonet, who followed him with his head down. It was starting to rain. I walked behind an assault sergeant, the kind with an armoured head and loopholes instead of eyes. He didn't talk much, understandably. His face had been modified to the point where his mouth was nothing but a badly drawn slot. It was a necessity that could not be eliminated, because he still needed to feed. He pointed the way to me with gestures. The rain was intensifying and the walls of the trenches were crumbling down like rye bread. As I waddled in the soaking mud I passed modified and unmodified men, staring at me with both repugnance and respect. To the lot of them we were new, different. We were the surprise factor, the one thing the Germans would not be expecting. We were the Barbed Wire.

I was confused by the subterraneous maze, and could hardly keep up with the sergeant. With every step my feet sunk into the mud, tripping over rats, live and dead alike. The rain was now a storm. The night was darkness. Perfect. The sergeant raised a hand and we stopped. There was my comrade. He would have gone unnoticed to anyone else, but I could sense the impossible contortion of barbed wire on the man whose hand I would soon be shaking.

I said goodbye to the sergeant and climbed a small wooden ladder to the exterior. I felt fear, of course. Panic. They could shoot me that very instant and I would not be able to do anything to avoid it. But nothing happened. It was the dead of night. It rained, and we all knew it was on those nights that the troops moved forward and the trench wars were flooded in mud and blood.

"Hello," said the other Barbed Wire.

"Hello," I whispered.

I shook his hand, before placing my body in a position that would have been impossible to another human being. Together we formed a barbed wire fence. I felt the spikes of my comrade's wires sinking into the palm of my hand. I felt the pain, the pain, a pain that would keep me alert and awake. Because they would be coming tonight. They would advance under cover of the darkness, of the rain. And there we would be, waiting.

Waiting to embrace them.

Translated by Alicia L. Alonso

The Unusual Commission

Beston Barnett

ON MY FIRST DAY PAINTING his portrait, the Vizconde de Abadón told me a story about the devil.

He began innocently enough, by asking if I was satisfied with my appointment as court painter. It was rare that one of my subjects would condescend to conversation during a sitting—particularly a grandee like the Vizconde—but this was an unusual commission.

"*Su Señoría.* I am, of course, honored to serve at the court of the Catholic King. I could not be other than satisfied."

The Vizconde seemed to mull over my answer. I had out my smallest brush—five delicate strands of squirrel hair—and was carefully touching in the details of his sleeve. Small black beads ran in rows down to frills at his cuff, and each had to be made to glint just so.

"*Service,* yes, but do you not take pleasure in the mixing of colors? The play of light? Do you not, perhaps, put something of yourself into each new painting? I ask from mere curiosity, of course."

Again, I felt wrong-footed. To what admission might this nobleman be leading me? Nor were *color* and *light* the current fashion in the portraiture of the Spanish court, where funereal tones and pale faces had become synonymous with piety. Given all that had been hinted about the Vizconde de Abadón, I was unsure what tone to adopt.

Dabbing at my palette, I replied, "My craft—including, as *su Señoría* says, the observing of color and light—is in service to the glory of the Lord and, by extension, the glory of the king and the commissions he gives me. I strive to hold up a mirror, nothing more. If something of myself shows in my paintings, then I apologize: it is a personal flaw in an otherwise God-given talent."

This was a more pompous response than I had meant to give. The Vizconde sounded amused.

"A talent given by... Him... as you say, but also, I presume, a talent earned by years of hard and patient study on your part? It's a mirror you hold up, is it? Hmmn. A mirror... You must be very talented indeed for his Catholic Majesty to appoint a *converso* as his court painter."

I gripped my brush. In these uncertain times, it is enough for the name of your great-great-grandmother to be found in a Jewish cemetery to rouse the Inquisition against you. But there seemed to be no threat in his voice, only an amused disdain: for myself or for the king, I could not tell.

I responded only, "As you say, *su Señoría.*"

To settle my nerves, I paused to mix another batch of *osso nero,* the paste of charred bone that the Italians employ so ingeniously to make black clothing stand out against a dark background. The smell of linseed oil bloomed between us.

"Do you know the story," began the Vizconde, "of the

man who, like you, kept a mirror in his bag? No? Picture a man, a clever man like yourself, walking the lonely road from somewhere to somewhere—let us say, Toledo to Cartagena, the road you've just travelled—when he is waylaid by the devil. This frightening creature waves its pitchfork and gnashes its teeth and snarls something ridiculous like, 'Aha! Now, I will eat your soul, puny mortal!'

"But the wily man replies, 'I am not frightened of you. I have fought and captured numerous devils. In fact, I have one here in my bag!'

"'Never!' cries the devil, waving his pitchfork and gnashing his teeth, 'Show me this supposed devil in your bag!' Whereupon, the man opens his bag with the mirror at its bottom, and the devil peers in and sees another devil much like himself there, waving its pitchfork and gnashing its teeth. And the poor devil takes fright and runs off!"

It was an unusual commission, received under unusual circumstances. Five days before, I had been working intently on a still life in the cramped studio provided for me beneath the palace, when with a bang, the door was flung open.

A voice barked, "The king approaches!"

I kneeled immediately, then risked a glance across the room to where my frail mother dozed under her quilt on a cot by the stove. I saw her startled eyes open, then sink closed in feigned sleep. The king rarely left his court, and when he did, only his most trusted advisors were allowed to look him in the face. My mother and I had both heard the rumors about the punishments meted out to those commoners who disobeyed.

What could possibly have brought the king himself to my studio? I held my breath and fixed my eyes on the floor.

"Painter!"

Here were the royal shoes, softest black leather and gold buckles, standing on the boards of my paint-spattered floor.

"*Su Majestad,*" I said quickly.

"Painter," the gold buckles boomed, "we require a portrait of the Vizconde de Abadón. See to it."

"Of course, *su Ma... su Católica Majestad,*" I stammered, "It is an honor to serve."

I remained on the floor, unmoving, but so did the gold-buckled shoes. Awkward seconds passed, and when he did speak again, a certain cunning had entered his voice.

"One more thing... You must not look at the portrait... Until we have viewed the finished portrait that you will paint, no one must see it. No one, not even yourself! Is that clear?"

"I..." Nothing was clear to me, but what else could I say? "...Of course, *su Majestad,* it will be as you wish."

With a martial stomp, the gold buckles turned and exited the room.

I glanced across at my mother and began, "What could tha—" but her darting eyes stopped me. I had failed to notice that some of the king's retinue remained. Looking up from my position on the floor, I recognized Yñigo, *consejero* to the king and ranking member of the Inquisition, a scheming, avaricious man with the bald head and wattles of a vulture, now flanked in my doorway by two liveried guards.

"Listen carefully, painter," said Yñigo in his cracked high whine. "The Vizconde whom you are to paint is an eccentric and possibly seditious man who harbors Moors in his guard and Jews in his treasury. He may make strange demands of you or tempt you with confidences. But you must insist that the king's instructions be followed to the letter. You are not to look at the portrait or allow anyone else to look at it. You are to keep it covered at all times. Do you understand?"

"I will, of course, *señor consejero,* but how... how can I paint a portrait if I cannot look at it?"

He dismissed my question with a flick of his veined hand. "You will think of some contrivance. Perhaps you can uncover only a small portion at a time. Now go, prepare your paints and canvas: you leave tonight. Abadón is three days journey into the mountains above Cartagena."

I recoiled. "The Vizconde is not here in Toledo? But, *señor,* I am terribly sorry, I cannot travel at this time. My mother is ill, and there is no one to take care of her just now. Her lungs—"

"As for your mother..." The *consejero*'s face lapsed into a cruel grin as he waved one of the guards towards her cot. "She will, of course, be cared for in your absence. Her residence with us will be an opportunity to clear up certain *irregularities* in your heritage. I am certain it can all be straightened out by the time you return with the portrait. *Completed* and *un-viewed.*"

The guards pulled my mother to her feet. They gave me no time to do more than wrap her shoulders in a quilt and kiss her forehead. She kept repeating "I'll be fine" between coughing fits as they led her from the room.

To this day, I have never felt so helpless.

On the second day of the painting of his portrait, the Vizconde de Abadón wore a hat of the modern sort called a *capitán* with a jaunty peacock feather captured in a silk band. The morning light was clean and buttery, and each downy plumule of the feather in the Vizconde's hat seemed aflame. There were so many colors! Despite my apprehensions about the strange circumstances and about my ailing mother, I was immersed in my work. I had a peacock feather to paint. And, after all, the only help it was in my power to offer my mother was through this painting.

The feather jiggled only slightly when the Vizconde spoke.

"Does the world seem fair to you, señor painter?"

"Su Señoría?"

"Is it fair, for example, that you must use the darker colors over and over again, but others—orange or turquoise—go almost untouched? Colors must have feelings too, no?" The Vizconde chuckled to himself, "So the Greeks tell us: green is jealous, yellow is afraid. Merely a fancy, of course, but can you not imagine them whispering among themselves in your satchel? Each yearning to be let loose, and the black always lording it over them?"

I *had* entertained similar fantasies and experienced now a distinct satisfaction in preparing some rarely used colors for the Vizconde's peacock feather. Hair-thin lines of pink and gold set off green waves of plumules and encircled the purple eye at the feather's end. There are certain arrangements of contrasting lines that, if stared at, induce a corresponding tremor in the viewer: a phantom vibration, as though the colors sing and shift. Something like that was taking place on the canvas now. But I did not choose to admit quite so much to the Vizconde, whose conversation I found unnerving.

So I said, "Perhaps the purpose of the more brilliant colors is to provide that dash of contrast which magnifies the solemnity of the blacks and umbers. In my work, I strive to include only that which magnifies the sanctity of His creation. I am hopeful that the colors themselves—should they suddenly find voice—would declare this purpose sufficient."

"You are a pious man, señor *converso,*" said the Vizconde, sounding annoyed. "And are the *comuneros* then content with their lot as the 'dash of contrast' to the military might of the king? Do the Moors who built his palaces and churches take pride in having provided a 'dash of contrast' to the Catholic Monarch as they are chased from Iberia? Do you baby-eating *conversos* enjoy being a 'dash of contrast' for the Inquisition? How far would you like me to extend the analogy?"

I was taken aback, both by the turn of his thoughts and his open disdain. On my guard, I said, "I apologize, su *Señoría*, I did not know we were speaking in analogies."

The Vizconde remained silent for some time, during which I shifted from working on his hat in the upper middle of the canvas to the area in the upper right-hand corner. In most portraits, this is a background of matte gray or, at most, a blurred suggestion of a landscape. But it was as if, now that the peacock colors had made their way onto my palette, they refused to be put away. Looking at the wall behind the Vizconde—a simple clay wall which the light hit obliquely—I saw the lumps and textures the trowel had left, and I saw also how these textures could be depicted as gradations of color: gray-green, gray-pink, gray-blue. Then too I saw that the light itself had color and even mass: a pure transparent yellow-orange that weighted the air. Perhaps something had gone wrong with my eyes, some brief clouding or excess of blood caused by the higher altitude, but even so, I wanted to capture it. I worked in haste, applying paint, scraping it away, applying it again.

"Do you know what the devil looks like?"

Surprised from my trance-like effort, I could not think what to say, but the Vizconde continued without waiting.

"I mean, as a painter: have you given any thought as to how you would paint the devil? You must have seen a Last Judgment or two; it seems every church must have one. A lot of reds and blacks and horns and hooves. And more of those ridiculous pitchforks. Maybe you have painted one yourself? No? Then listen, I will tell you another story.

"Two tenant farmers work neighboring acres outside a village in—let's say—Cádiz. Each has a wife and three children, each works hard to keep food on their table, though the landlord takes most of their harvests. One might assume these similar farmers would share similar fates. Yet on a certain night, farmer number one is gifted a dream, while farmer number two sleeps undisturbed. Only number one dreams that, beneath a certain tree in the nearby forest, a treasure lies buried.

"Now, does that seem fair to you? How did... He... decide which of the two farmers should receive this fantastic dream? Or is it possible that dreams are not His purview, but the Devil's?

"Rhetorical, I know," apologized the Vizconde, "I'm being rhetorical. At any rate, farmer number one proceeds into the forest with a spade and returns with a sack full of gold. His dream comes true! No dream for farmer number two, though. He will have to continue toiling away for the landlord while farmer number one lives in luxury. When number two gets the news, he pretends congratulations, but underneath he is consumed with envy, and that night he begins plotting how to take the gold for himself. He remembers a costume he wore in the Carnaval parade some years past—a devil costume—and he finds it still folded in his wife's blanket chest.

"So, late in the night, he creeps to the house of farmer number one disguised as the devil, scares the family just enough to keep them from putting up a fight, and steals the gold. At home, farmer number two is just congratulating himself on a theft well executed when a dismaying problem arises. He cannot remove the disguise.

"Can you spot the *so-called* moral? The devil costume: it has become part of the thief. It cannot be removed!"

The Vizconde sounded almost bitter. Perhaps the story

meant something different to him than it did to me.

I may have been distracted. My experiments in color felt both fruitful and necessary, but they were dangerous, for myself and my mother. I told myself that the king would surely overlook any aberrations in a corner of the portrait if the facial features at its center were striking enough. But at this point, I could only hope that my subject had such striking features.

After two days of painting his portrait, I had yet to see the Vizconde's face.

———◆·◆———

The road to Abadón had been long and anxious, laden as I was with worries about my mother and about the portentous commission I had been given. It rained much of the time. And at each inn or market where we stopped, I heard the name of the Vizconde de Abadón—unknown to me days before—whispered in the most outlandish rumors.

"Abadón is funding the *comuneros.*"

"Abadón has declared against the *comuneros.*"

"Abadón keeps a Moorish guard, not of *moriscos* but of warriors from the Golden Horde."

"Abadón is a kabbalist who brings clay to life and speaks to the dead."

"Abadón cheats at cards."

After a misty afternoon traveling by cart up into the Sierra Béjerit, I came at last to the fertile plateau of Abadón itself and was met after nightfall at the gate of a large compound by an aged but incredibly muscular African dwarf—Dbala by name—who hoisted my satchel and bag as though they weighed nothing and led me across empty but well-kept grounds and a wide torch-lit courtyard to a small windowless room like a larder at the bottom of a flight of stone steps.

"The Vizconde will see you shortly," said this formidable little person in a deep, accent-less Castilian. And then he left me to wait alone.

I was frightened, of course. I was in a small dark room in a country far from my own, awaiting a man of outsized legend, and I would have to explain to this man that I must paint his portrait without looking at it. At best, I could hope for incredulity. At worst?

My imagination balked.

When I had been sitting for some time in the dark, a flicker of candlelight approached the doorway, and then the Vizconde himself entered the room and settled onto the stone bench opposite.

He sat there before me, clearly a man; I could make out muddy black shoes and a fine wool coat. I could even make out the long fingers that supported the candlestick. But he held it before him in such a way as to always interpose the flame perfectly between my eyes and his face, so that just where I would have liked to look I was instead blind.

At first, not understanding his purpose, I instinctively dodged my head to see around the flame. But his placement of the candle was unerring. All I saw of his head and shoulders was a bright blur which, when I looked down and away, became a dark purple sunspot shuddering across the stone floor.

"So, court painter..." His voice was refined but not frightening, and pitched like a tenor's, not the voice one would expect of a kabbalist sorcerer or a commander of the Golden Horde. "The king has commanded my portrait. How... flattering? Yes, I suppose I must be flattered. Are you also flattered to be given this commission halfway across the country? Yes? No? Well, you must be tired from your long journey. I'll have Dbala find you a room. Unless the king demands we begin immediately?"

I had not yet become accustomed to the Vizconde's provocative manner—in fact, I never did. He spoke as if we were not noble and commoner, but simply two strangers sharing an amusing joke at the world's expense. Between his over-familiarity and the effect of the candle, I was wholly disconcerted. I could only remind myself that, in this circumstance, I was a tool of the king, nothing more.

I said, "Thank you for the gracious welcome, *su Señoría.* If it pleases you, I would be happy to begin tomorrow. The king did, however, give me some special instructions regarding the portrait. Neither you nor I is to look at the painting during or after its completion."

At this, the Vizconde stiffened. I could not make out his expression, but his body seemed suddenly alert, and he gave a few small intakes of breath, like a hound sniffing a fox in the wind.

"I propose to work on small sections only," I said into the silence, "while keeping the rest of the painting covered. It will be a challenge to achieve continuity across the sections, but I believe it can be done."

After a moment, he said, "And do you know the reason for the king's... injunction?"

"I would not presume to—"

"Of course you would not, señor painter, of course you would not." The Vizconde's amused manner returned. "Well, I shall willingly comply with the king's injunction. And, if you will suffer me to do so, good court painter, I shall impose an injunction of my own. Just as you will only work on one small section of the painting at a time, so shall I only reveal one small section of myself at a time. I envision a kind of scaffolding supporting a frame sectioned into twelve squares—three across and four down, yes?—each with a screen that can be raised or lowered to reveal a different part of me, and this frame matches the proportions of a series of twelve covers which you hang on your easel, each cover corresponding to one of the open screens. Dbala is a masterful carpenter; you and he can work out the details in the morning. Do you accept this challenge, court painter?"

Another difficulty added to an already difficult project: my mind spun. But as I pictured it, what he described sounded much like the method the old masters used to reproduce a large mural from a drawing. A small grid on the sketch, a larger but proportionate grid on the wall; I had used the technique more than once during my apprenticeship. And what choice did I have? I had to return with this portrait to free my mother.

"I shall endeavor to comply with your request, *su Señoría.*"

"Ha! Very good! And of course you would not *presume* to ask me the reasons for my further injunction?"

I felt mocked and cowed and far from home. I could no longer bear to stare into that candle flame, but said, "No, *su Señoría,* " diplomatically, with my eyes on my feet.

The Vizconde stood to leave, but turned for a last word.

"I shall volunteer a partial explanation nonetheless. The candle and the screens are for your own protection, señor painter. I can conceive of a day when you may wish to honestly deny that you ever laid eyes on the Vizconde de Abadón."

———————

Dbala proved indispensable. That first morning, we built a stretcher for my canvas and then a larger frame of the same proportions behind which the Vizconde would be screened. The room we occupied was grand, an empty refectory with big south-facing windows and high ceilings. While I began mixing paints, he stitched sackcloth veils for the frame and for my canvas, the latter with square windows cut out that would allow me to uncover one section at a time. By trial-and-error—the dwarf balancing on a stack of books to impersonate the Vizconde—we found the proper placement for the easel and screen, then marked the floor where I was to stand so as to ensure a repeatable line of sight.

The first sitting began that afternoon. I was to work for three days, finishing three squares the first day, six, the second, and the last three on the third morning. We agreed on a system: when Dbala told me the Vizconde was waiting outside our makeshift studio, I would place my feet over the mark on the floor and close my eyes, then Dbala would invite his master to assume his pose, and then Dbala would ring a little bell he kept on his person, indicating that I could begin. I would open my eyes to stare through one window in a three-by-four grid, revealing an elbow or a hat or a knee. At the end of the session, we would repeat the same formula in reverse: first the little bell, then I closed my eyes, then Dbala invited his master to retire and told me when he had gone. When I was ready to switch between one section and the next, Dbala would first close the open veil and then open the next one I indicated. In this way we made steady progress, never taking a break (which must have been difficult on the Vizconde's joints) and never being interrupted. Somehow, the incomparable Dbala also found time to make and serve my meals, iron my clothes, shine my boots, and clean my room. He was the only servant—in fact, the only other person—that I ever saw while in Abadón.

To achieve a continuity of light, I mostly worked on the lower squares in the afternoons and the upper squares in the mornings. I skipped around a bit though, either because I had been infected by the storybook quality of the project or simply to keep my eyes fresh. But something strange was happening to my vision.

I painted in my usual way that first afternoon,

experiencing only a subtle heightening of my senses, brought on—I thought—by the rare focus which the lack of interruptions and the privacy of the screen afforded me. But during the second day, and specifically after I started on that peacock feather, I started to see color as I had not before, and to feel a kind of desperation to explore its possibilities. Yet I knew I was endangering my livelihood and my mother. After that second day—after what may have been the most exciting work day of my life—I was exhausted, elated, confused, and near prostrate with anxiety. The painting was three quarters done, yet how frustrating not to be able to look at it whole and assess my success or failure! I vowed to paint more conservatively the next day.

On that third and last morning, I rose early, ate the spiced egg left out for me, and was standing on my mark, palette in hand, when Dbala entered the refectory. I had the left leg, the right arm, and the face still to paint. Some minutes later, he informed me that the master waited outside. I closed my eyes, and after a pause, Dbala's little bell rang.

Then it was as if I opened my eyes from within a rainbow. Here was the black stocking of the Vizconde—his calf, his foot: a common limb I had painted a hundred times—and yet that black contained every color, a war of colors. And though, distantly, I recognized that I was endangering the project, I could not help but try and get this war of colors down on canvas. In truth, I was desperate to do so. Abandoning sketching and underpainting, I began to work the paint wetly on, mixing right on the canvas, forcing wet paint into wet paint.

An hour later, I stood back and blinked. It looked right. Wrong but right. I had painted not what was there to the eye exactly, but what was more than there. Some rational part of me must have seen that I had painted not a boot but a goat's

hoof, yet I could not, would not undo the work. I was frantic
to begin the next square.

When I called, "Next!" to Dbala, the Vizconde burst
out laughing behind the screen.

"Señor painter, you may be the most incurious man I
have ever met. A *hoof,* and he keeps on painting without a
mumble!"

"Su Señoría."

I answered by instinct alone. The rest of me was
transfixed. With the next window open, the Vizconde's
right arm and chest were revealed, and the rainbows of my
earlier vision were intact or even intensified. But now I felt
that they said something, that they called out to be heard.
There was rage in the red highlights off the beads of his vest,
and great sorrow in the curve of his long-nailed fingers.
Tenderness and wrath and melancholy, all braided together.
A mother's love, a man's hatred of his oppressor. The very
air, the very light cried out the injustices in the world, the
beautiful meaningless suffering. Pathos, color, story,
beauty, truth. I had to paint it. I could not really attend to
what the Vizconde said next, yet some part of me must have
heard his words and recorded them, for they returned to me
later with uncomfortable clarity.

He said, "Have you not at least wondered why all this
business with the screens and the veils is necessary? You
might dismiss me as a provincial eccentric, but the king? Do
you not wonder why he has never commissioned a portrait of
himself? Why it should be a capital offence to look upon his
face? No?

"He gives credence perhaps to the old superstition
which associates possessing an image of a person with
having power over that person. If I have a picture of you or
even draw a picture of you, then I can, in some mystical
sense, own you. But if others have that picture of you as

well, then my ownership is diminished and my power over you is reduced. Better to have the only picture, and better still to be the only one who has ever seen it.

"Scholars trace this particular line of superstition back to an ancient alchemists' legend about the devil: he who possesses a likeness of the devil *in his true form* can command the devil to do his bidding. Like Solomon commanded the army of djinn. And this idea of the 'true form' is important because the devil, it is said, is most often in disguise. It would seem ridiculous for *su Católica Majestad* to believe such a thing, much less for him to believe that one of his lowly vassals was that very infernal creature. Honestly, I can't imagine who starts these rumors..."

He chuckled and then continued in a lower register. "But I tell you this, my friend. There is an older legend. A legend from the making of the world. And it says that the man who looks deliberately upon the true form of the devil—not the snake or the goat's head, but the true complete form of the fallen angel—that man dies. *In terror.* "

I can only imagine the effect that these words might have had on me, had I been there to hear them. But I was not there, not really. I was an eye and a hand and a paintbrush alone with the great living canvas of the world in which all was color and pattern and violent tenderness and radiant misery and every particle in the universe sang out, *Death to the tyrant!*

In a state of ecstasy, I held my brush aloft and called "Next!" to Dbala, then turned, eager in every fiber to confront at last the face of the Vizconde.

The return trip to Toledo passed in a blur. My conscious thoughts were mostly with my mother: what I could do for her when she was released to me, what doctors we might see, whether she might be well enough to travel. But beneath those concerns ran a vast undercurrent of feeling which must have always been within me, building up unacknowledged and now loosed somehow by the colors I had been shown. There seemed so much injustice in the world. So much went unanswered. What self-respecting man, I thought bitterly, would aspire to work for an authority which despised his people and mistreated his family?

And all that trip, the portrait of the Vizconde, rolled and wrapped in velvet, travelled beside me like a fizzing cannon. I did not think on what it might portray.

Arriving, I went first to the headquarters of the Inquisition, situated just far enough from the palace to shield royal ears from the screaming. I was told that my mother was poorly, but that she was eating, and that I could not visit her without the signature of the *consejero*. I was given an order to be signed.

From there I went to the court and announced myself. After a short wait, I was shown directly to the royal apartments, the canvas and easel carried under my arm. I was halfway through setting up the viewing when the king, the *consejero,* and two more guards trooped in. I fell to the floor.

"So, it is done! You have completed the portrait of Abadón?"

"Yes, *su Majestad.*"

"And you were able to produce this without looking at it?" There was naked greed in the king's voice. "Has anyone else seen it?"

"No one has seen it, *su Majestad,* not even myself." I stood, careful to face away from the king, and finished clipping the canvas and its velvet cover to the easel. My hands shook.

"Well done. Now leave me. All of you!"

The guards and I hurried from the room, our eyes averted. But the *consejero* held back.

"I should stay, *su Majestad.* I can help you verify the authenticity of—"

"Be gone, Yñigo!"

Coming through the doors to find us waiting outside, the *consejero* screeched, "Get away from here! Go and guard something else!" Then rushed around the corner himself. The guards marched off in the opposite direction, but I followed him with the release order in my hand. I found him surreptitiously pulling aside a tapestry where I guessed he must have a peephole into the royal apartments. He did not like being caught.

"Get away from here, painter!"

"Please, *señor,* my mother's release. I have finished the portrait as promised."

"I said get away!"

But I would not go, and there were no guards to make me. I held out plume and ink. His eyes darted behind the tapestry and back to me.

"Insolence," he spat and took the plume and signed.

I hurried from the palace and retrieved my mother. It was a happy reunion, but anxious: she was painfully thin and still wracked with coughing. I could only pray to... Whomever... that she would be strong enough.

My bag and my paints were already packed. By nightfall, we were leagues from the city.

———✦———

What caused the 1521 burning of Toledo remains a mystery, though blame is generally placed with the *comuneros.* Only about a third of the walled city actually burned, but that included the palace and surrounding government buildings, where the royal family, the court, the guard, and most of the inquisitors of Toledo are assumed to have died. No one survived who witnessed their deaths.

But I can picture them, and have, over and over again these many years, largely without remorse. I imagine the king uncovering my painting, stepping back, and greed turning to terror as he falls to the floor clutching his heart. I cannot picture his face because I was never allowed to look at it, but I can clearly imagine the face of the *consejero* pressed to a peephole in the wall, suddenly transfixed, his rheumy eyes wide. He soils himself, claws at the dark tapestry, and dies in his own filth.

Then hours or even days pass before someone has the temerity to knock at the doors of the royal apartments and, receiving no reply, to enter. Perhaps a guard or a mistress, perhaps even some member of the royal family whose portrait I had once painted: the queen or the *infantes.* Seeing the king on the floor, examining the body, how could they not then glance up at the easel so conspicuously set in the center of the room and find my Vizconde smiling back at them?

And so the corpses pile up. And each time someone enters, another is added to the pile, falling before the easel in terror and in the stench of death. How high might the pile have grown before a superstitious visitor would not enter that doomed apartment, but, fearing contagion, set it aflame?

I take no pride in my involvement. A small blow to the Catholic Monarchy and to the Inquisition. Their stranglehold on my native country continues unabated, oppressing *conversos* and *moriscos* and *comuneros* alike. It was a gesture, ultimately futile.

My mother passed away some years ago. We had fled to Livorno in Italy and hidden for a few months before crossing the Mediterranean to settle in Tunis. Here the Jews are taxed disproportionately and the language is strange, but at least our community is treated with a measure of respect. In her last years, she often remarked how much she liked my new paintings, mostly flower arrangements in restrained explosions of color, though I also paint shop signs and ornamental ceilings—there are many such commissions in Tunis. Her appreciation meant a great deal to me, because, in leaving the king's service, our circumstances were much reduced.

I seek out color now, but avoid lushness, choosing instead the small spray of hibiscus, the geometrical figure, the walled garden. I fear most that my restraint may slip, that I may find myself painting again—feverishly—a horn or a cloven hoof.

As for portraits, I have never painted another.

Scent

Maria Haskins

HER CABINET is full of perfumes, and the scents try to escape as soon as I open the door—twined tendrils reaching out—each scent a murmur, a ripple of memory beneath my skin. There are liquid amber and fluid gold, swirling ruby and molten jade, lustrous indigo and glossy lilac—gleaming prisms of crystal and glass, stoppers carved into birds and beasts and blossoms—all aglow in her gloomy boudoir, lit only by the flames beneath the copper cauldron in the other room.

"Don't touch, Alynna."

Mother's voice. Not loud or sharp, because Mother never raises her voice. But firm. Like the hand on my shoulder, turning me around, away.

She asks me to brush her hair, as she has done every night for as long as I dare remember. I unravel her waist-long braid, brushing black tresses into silk and shadow, her skin already warm and flushed in the heat and steam rising from the deep basin cut into the stone floor.

The golden mirror holds Mother's reflection. She is so beautiful that it hurts even me to look at her: beauty like a blade—a sleek, perfect edge—sliding through skin and ribs so easily you barely notice when it stops your heart. I don't want to look, but I inhale her scent with each sweep of the brush: the smell of spring mornings in the garden, days when she'd hold my hand, bedtimes when she kissed me. Each brushstroke tangling into memory.

Don't touch.

In the other room, the fire keeps the water boiling, heating the large transparent sphere suspended on its chain above the cauldron. Inside the glass, the heated fluids rise, trickling slowly through twisting tubes of copper, dripping into vials. Something twitches within the steam and mist and glass. I do not wish to see. Not tonight.

She rises from the chair, and the weakest part of me wishes that she would stay this way: that she would not undress, not step into the steaming water, not wash and rinse her skin. I breathe in her scent, trying to hold on to it, keep it safe, forever. Mother, safe, forever.

The gown drops, embroidered silk blazing blue and black like butterfly wings, smooth brown skin beneath.

Through the window beyond her naked form, I glimpse the forest: trees, the moon, narrow trails made by paws and hooves beneath shriveled leaves and twisted boughs. There is a way through the shadows and the mires. Maybe a bird could fly above. Maybe a wolf could find the trail. But I have no wings, no fur, no beak, no snout. I have only a child's hands, scarred and calloused. Strong enough to carry water and light the fire, to brush Mother's hair, and lay out the gowns upon the bed. Not strong enough to break open locks, or crack the wood that bars the door.

Don't touch.

Once, I touched. Once, I balanced on a stool, reaching into the cabinet, my hand trembling so it almost knocked the bottles over. I took the vial on the highest shelf, in the farthest corner, the one with the carved onyx stopper, wings spread in flight, black feathers carved into the stone. I removed the stopper, didn't let the liquid touch my skin, only breathed: felt the shiver of beak and flight.

That bottle isn't there anymore. Perhaps it's locked in the chest next to her bed, buried beneath pearl-embroidered lace and silver-stitched brocades.

I watch her descend into the scalding water, watch her wash Mother off her flesh and bones with oil and soap and sponge, shedding scent and memories, skin and spirit, until she is twisted spines and cracked hide, gut-rip claws, and needle fangs, red tongue flickering between. The water fills the crooks and crevices of her body, rinsing warped limbs stitched together by sinew, spell, and shadow. She rises, stripped of all illusion. Clean. Strong as roots and vines, as tooth and bone.

In the other room, the glass sphere glistens, tarnished with dark residue above the roiling water. I smell wolf tonight. By now I can tell the smells apart: the animals and birds, the children, the women and the men, the tiny faeries with wings of spun gold, the beasts of horn and wing and tusk. Each trapped inside the sphere, above the heat; giving up its scent and spirit, releasing the essence hid within as the bonds of life are loosened. Only the dregs are left behind, slick and foul, to scrub and clean, leaving my palms and fingers raw.

Don't touch.

A crooked talon strokes my hair, slides down my cheek, cutting into skin and flesh.

"Alynna, give her to me."

She takes the bottle filled only yesterday from my hand,

contents shimmering like liquid strawberries and honey: the girl with red hair, barely older than I am, eyes like moss and water. Mouth open, but bereft of sound as she lay inside the glass, as the heat drew out every last bit of her. Her essence held in crystal now, a crimson stopper to keep her in her place.

One splash, two, of strawberry and honey. Firm flesh and creamy skin blushed with fire flows over stripped bones and creaking joints, eyes like moss and water open, red-brass curls tumble down her back.

"You will be gorgeous one day, won't you?" There is a gleam of hidden teeth and darkness as she speaks. "Make your Mother proud."

I think of black feathers stirring, claws and beak, and I nod.

A Light in the Darkness

Gary Buller

I'D ALL BUT LOST HOPE when I saw a light in the darkness. I raised my lantern, shielding my eyes against the downpour and squinted in an effort to see the source of the flickering, orange flame. A granite building nestled within the moorland hills, all but camouflaged by the elements. Its roof was grey slate upon which moss clung like barnacles to the bough of a ship, and the walls appeared ghostly blue.

I unrolled the map and attempted to pinpoint my location, turning full circle and taking in the contours of land. It was useless. I cursed my so-called friend, Hubert Cockforster for cancelling our hiking trip and my own damned stubbornness for embarking regardless. A cruel wind howled, whipping the wet grass against my knees and soaking my trousers. My fingers were prune-like and numb. I was hungry and in dire need of shelter. Pocketing the map and keeping my head low, I strode toward the light.

Upon closer inspection, the building appeared to be a repurposed farmhouse. A dry-stone wall surrounded it and there was a coach house adjacent. The gates rusted on their hinges and were overgrown with weeds. A sign squeaked as it swung in the wind, suspended by chains from a wooden post. When I shone my lantern upon it, the words painted in white were barely visible

THE SNAKE INN.

A brass lamp hung above the entrance and illuminated the yard, the resulting shadows dancing and weaving about my feet. It was then I felt unseen eyes upon me. Looking to one of the windows I saw movement as a shape slid from view. Gooseflesh puckered along my arms. *Don't be silly,* I told myself. *It's nothing but a draft agitating the curtains.* It was cold, dark and I needed rest. Raising my hand, I rapped my knuckles on the hardwood door.

Presently an old man answered, holding a candle high. A gown overhung his pajamas and strands of silver hair protruded from a tasseled nightcap. He looked me up and down, as if surprised by my intrusion, and his blue eyes glistened like sapphires.

"Can I help you, sir?" he said.

"Sorry if I woke you and your good lady at such a late hour," I replied. "I'm in need of supper and lodgings for the night. Are you open for business?"

"Alas, I have no wife and my sister is no longer with us. You are welcome to a room, though. Take your pick."

He stood to the side and gestured for me to enter. The interior was blessedly warm. A passage led to a large tap-room with a roaring fire. The walls were whitewashed and decorated with brass ornaments and faded oil paintings. The old man took his place behind the bar. He blew the dust from the cover of a weighty leather volume and pushed it in my direction.

"The guest book." He said, by way of explanation. "I don't normally entertain such formalities, but the law is the law."

I opened to the bookmark. The pages were yellow with age and blackened along one edge. The previous guest, a Mister T. Smyth from Royton, had stayed at the inn for three nights, but I was surprised to see the date was five years prior. A little perplexed, but not wishing to be impolite, I filled out my details, signed my name and returned the volume without comment.

"That'll be tenpenny, sir," the landlord said. "That includes food, ale and the room."

I handed him the coins from my purse, removed my rucksack and took a seat by the fire. There were six tables set about the taproom, all empty. Above the mantelpiece, an impressive buck surveyed us, the gaps between his antlers bridged by spiderwebs. His fur was sooty and singed. I held my hands out to the flames, allowing the warmth to breathe life into my torpid fingers and marveling at the steam rising from my garments.

Soon enough the old man brought two flagons of ale, two bowls and a crust of bread on a tray.

"Would you mind some company?" he asked. "It's been a while."

"Not at all." I said.

He set the tray on an upturned barrel and invited me to take a drink. The ale was rich and brown with a full body. It tasted both sweet and smoky. A simmering pot hung above the fire, and the old man filled our bowls with a ladle.

"How long have you been landlord here?" I asked.

"Twenty years," said he, handing me a bowl. I took a mouthful. It was delicious. "Lydia and I did a brisk trade with the cotton merchants. It seems only yesterday this very room was hazy with pipe smoke and filled with laughter and music." His expression dimmed. "Then the new road was built. It took a heavy toll. Lydia spent most of the time in her quarters, occasionally ringing for food or water, but she barely touched her plate. The solitude was enough to drive a man mad."

I paused mid-chew and looked to the rafters. A strange sound, like a medicine ball rolling across bare boards travelled from North to South across the space above us. The old man fixed his eyes on me.

"Pay no mind." He said. "This place is older than the hills. Like my good self, it is full of sighs and groans."

"Of course." I smiled, attempting to thaw his icy expression.

Thud.

Another sound, heavy and padded descended from the same room. A breath caught in my throat and despite the warmth I shivered. The old man maintained eye contact with me, but distaste twisted his lips into a sneer.

"Sighs and groans," he repeated.

The rest of the meal was a little awkward but uneventful. We spoke in trivialities, gazing into the flames. The old man offered me a second ale, but I declined, explaining it had been a long and stressful day. He poured himself another and downed it in one before leading me from the room. We climbed a flight of stairs, and I couldn't help but note their peculiar construction. Half the gradual incline consisted of angular, wooden steps, the other half a smooth slope-like surface. When I asked my host about them, he said, "My sister," and offered nothing more.

On the landing, the rain redoubled its efforts, tapping relentlessly on the window panes. The first-floor hallway was a long and claustrophobic space. Light from my host's candle spilled over dark wall panels and across a threadbare, burgundy carpet. The air was saturated by a strangely bitter odour, as out of place as it was familiar.

"Can you smell burning?"

The old man stopped in his tracks and fixed me with a look. His face was a mass of wrinkles, a vegetable left too long in the sun.

"No, sir. Perhaps it's tobacco? I partake occasionally, as did Lydia until the black lung took her."

"No, not tobacco. I can't put my finger on it."

The old man shrugged. He stopped by one of the doors and opened it, offering me a side glance which suggested he doubted my senses. I started to feel a little foolish. Did I really smell smoke? Perhaps it was tobacco after all. I needed a good night's sleep. Then my host did a very strange thing; he looked up and down the passageway before stepping close enough to smell the ale on his breath.

"The Inn is very old, and the floors aren't what they used to be," he whispered. "Please stay in your room whilst its dark. It's dangerous. There's a chamber pot under the bed and a bell on the side table should you need me."

I lit my lantern, thanked the old man and watched as he shuffled off into the shadows. Inside, the guest-room was modest but tidy with a single bed, a wardrobe, two chairs, a side table and of course, a chamber pot. As promised, a bell resided on the side table, its handle tied with ribbon. A bay window offered a wonderful view of the hills, and as I admired the scenery a fork of lightning licked the clouds.

The air was somewhat colder than the tap-room. I lit a fire in the hearth, pulled a chair close and draped my still-damp clothes over it, stripping down to my underwear. Retrieving the map from my rucksack, I climbed under the sheets and examined the lay of the land as the winds rattled the panes.

I traced a finger along the hills and forests to a place called Gaster. The *George and Dragon* was listed there, as was the *Hare and Hounds Inn* in the neighboring Hamlet of Midhope. I was almost certain of my approximate location, but *The Snake Inn* was not recorded anywhere in the vicinity. Surely such an old building should be present on a map of not more than a year old?

A sound rose, barely audible above the storm. I froze, cocked my head and strained my ears. For a long moment, nothing. Then I heard it again. The tinkle of a bell. I put the map aside, climbed out of bed and placed an ear to the door. Somewhere out in the passageway or one of the guest rooms, a bell rang once and then twice more, so low as to be almost inaudible. Was it my host's sister? Another guest? It would explain so much, but my gut instincts told me I was very much alone in this place.

Perhaps the old man was lonely or eccentric, I thought. Perhaps he was amusing himself at my expense by creating mischief in the dark. It didn't make an ounce of sense though; the old man had made his exit in one direction and the call of the bell came from another. With blood whooshing in my ears like a damned whirlpool, I took my lantern and thrust it out into the hallway, recalling the old man's warning not to leave my quarters. I held the light high, pointing it this way and that, chasing shadows into corners but saw nothing.

Just then, lightning flickered. A silhouette stood by the window at the far end of the hallway, black against white, an elongated shadow tattooed upon the carpet. It was there for but a second before darkness encroached once more. Thunder rolled across the hills and the building trembled. I aimed my lantern in that direction, took a step out of the room and peered into the darkness.

"Hello," I called. "Landlord?"

No reply came. Barefoot, and in my Long Johns, I carefully crept along the floorboards. The smell of blackened and burned wood grew with each step and I shielded my nose with the back of my hand.

The far end of the corridor was unoccupied, but I saw no door or any other means of exit. I was relieved and confused in equal measure. Here, a window overlooked the rear of the property. There was a stable, choked by ivy and with its door hanging from one bleeding hinge. The yard before it was cracked and full of weeds, sprigs of deer-grass protruding from the gravel. Rain over-spilled the guttering in heavy waterfalls, and deep puddles formed at the foot of the building.

A floorboard creaked at my back. I spun on my heels to see a light at the opposite end of the corridor, no bigger or brighter than a match. It bobbed from left to right, rising and falling with an unseen gait. It vanished into one of the rooms and was followed by another sound; the plaintive sobbing of a woman. Ice-water traced a line down my spine, but I felt compelled and duty bound to investigate. Perchance the old man was more eccentric or insidious than I thought.

Guided by the sobs, I retraced my steps, past the stairway, my guest room and to the opposite end of the passage. There I found one of the doors ajar, and it was from the darkness within the sounds came. I took a few deep breaths of acrid air and pushed the door, allowing it to swing inwards.

This guest room was much like my own, except the hearth was unlit and wispy clouds of breath spilled between my lips. A woman sat in a wheelchair facing the window. She wore a silken dress which might have been black or grey, and rested her head in her hands. Her shoulders shook with grief.

"Hello?" I ventured. "Apologies for intruding, but is all well?"

She didn't seem to hear, or was too deep in her melancholy to acknowledge my presence. I stepped inside and rested my lantern on the side table.

"My lady?"

I approached, extending a hand. My fingers plunged into a pool of air so frigid it burned. The woman raised her head and turned to look at me. At that moment I swear my heart stopped.

Her face was a mass of purple-black flesh punctuated by flecks of white. Her nose was gone and in its place two little holes laboured to draw air. Lips receded from her gums, exposing broken teeth in a permanent grimace. Only her eyes were unharmed, glinting like blue marbles in her charred sockets.

"Help Me," she hissed. "Please... Help Me."

A claw extended, and I withdrew, appalled by the thought of her touch. Her limbs were contorted where muscles had stiffened to piano-wire tightness and she stood and moved with the rigidity of a porcelain doll. I groaned, covering my mouth before a scream escaped. She smelled like overcooked bacon. No one should bear such injuries and live, I thought. It was impossible.

I withdrew from the room, away from my pursuer and backed into something which was not there before. I turned to find the old man blocking my way. His appearance was vastly different to our previous discourse.

Flaps of skin oozed from his face like molten wax, overhanging his nose and chin in thick globules. His mouth was all but melded shut and he produced a terrifying, keening whine from the holes which remained. His hands, both a mash of cremated flesh and exposed knuckles pressed upon my shoulders, forcing me down and onto the floor. His eyes were lidless and impossibly wide. *How dare you,* they said. *How dare you leave your room.* Now I knew why.

They both converged on me. I opened my mouth, tried to draw breath but found only thick, choking smoke. They reached down with misshapen hands and pinned me to the carpet, the cold miasma radiating from their bodies burning my skin and scorching my vision white. I tried to scream, tried to shout for help but my lungs were tight and heavy. I floundered within their grip like a grounded fish. Their disfigured masks loomed large, filling my vision, suffocating my world as flames licked around them like halos. Then mercifully, my world faded to grey.

Something rough and dry passed over my cheek, rousing me from unconsciousness.

"What's that Scout?" A voice asked. "What have you found there?"

The head of a man appeared above the long grass, concern etched on his face. He wore a deerstalker and sported a bushy moustache that quivered like a small animal as he spoke.

"My goodness, sir. Are you okay?"

He ambled over, through the uneven heather and knelt at my side. Scout, a blonde Labrador paused in his exploration to watch with interest. Lifting me into a sitting position the man produced a hip-flask from his inside jacket pocket and tilted the neck to my lips. The brandy spilled down my throat and blossomed in my stomach with a not unpleasant heat.

"What happened?" He asked. "And why in blazes are you in your underwear in this godforsaken place? Good job Scout here had his senses about him."

I wore naught but my Long-John's and we sat within the footings of a derelict building. The remnants of a dry-stone wall crumbled around us, and beyond, the uneven moorland hills reached to a grey sky.

"Where are we?" I asked, struggling to raise my voice above a hoarse whisper. "What is this place?" Vague but disturbing images swam about my head, images which later clarified into horrific focus.

"Snake Pass, if you must know," the gentleman said. "We're about ten miles away from Ashopton. If you want a more precise answer, we're amongst the ruins of the old Snake Inn."

I looked to him with disbelief, and my already frigid body shook vigorously.

"I used to stop here for the odd tipple," he continued, "until it burned to the ground back in '08. Rumours suggest the landlord started a fire in the upstairs hallway, retired to his quarters, and waited to die. Business went south you see—after the main road was built."

"'08," I murmured. "Five years ago."

"The fire lit up the hills from miles around. Some say they heard his sister screaming. She was an invalid and couldn't escape. Poor soul."

Scout trotted happily amongst the crumbling stone and blackened wood, sniffing in nooks and crannies. The man pocketed the hip-flask and lifted me to my feet, draping my arm around his neck.

"Let's get you home, then," he said.

I couldn't help but steal a final look at the space where an Inn once stood. Amongst the mounds of rubble and charred beams I spotted a rotten stable door, reclaimed by the ivy. Next to it, something protruded from the heather. Blackened, leather handles and a varnished, wooden backrest.

"We better get a move on, old boy," the man said, as the first drops of rain kissed my shoulders. "It would seem a storm is brewing."

The Cheshire's Grin

Irene Punti

PLINIUS HAS TURNED today's assembly into sheer torture with his speech. Many at the Comitium have become fascinated by the hem of their togas or, in Silianus' case, by his signet ring.

"How can such a bore have produced such a fine daughter?" my friend Manius whispers to me.

I shrug. Indeed, Aemilia is the most beautiful among the city maids. As blue-eyed and languid as a Siamese cat, her skin as pale and smooth as blancmange. But Manius knows I've never set great store by feminine beauty, and I've never seen Aemilia display any wit or talent beyond physical grace–although I can't fail to commiserate with her for having such an overbearing father.

Once again, Aemilia has rejected the invitation to my start-of-Festival banquet. A pity, although I sent it in jest more than anything else. The presence of Plinius' daughter in one of my banquets (even if she chose to remain fully clothed and boringly sober) would be the talk of the city for months.

But I wouldn't call Plinius a bore. I enjoy watching my fellow citizens squirm on the Comitium's stone seats, and I hadn't seen our Master of Cultural Artefacts tread on so many sandaled toes since he proposed that we take up the Roman custom of allowing masters to liberate their slaves.

"Even if only one or two Cheshire slaves in a generation were liberated, this would give the rest something to aspire to," said Plinius, wandering perilously close to the precipice. The idea of a Cheshire becoming a citizen is so abhorrent that we knew it would never prosper, but still we were shocked that Plinius dared suggest it. "It may forestall any potential uprisings, and at the very least, it would reduce violence during the Vanishing Festival," he argued. "Think of the lives that could be spared!"

No one doubts that Plinius is the most knowledgeable among us when it comes to the Roman Ideal, and yet we all agree that he's never managed to truly grasp it: We love the Festival exactly the way it is.

That's why today we're so impatient. We just wanted him to say that the smoke bombs have been installed and we could go ahead with the Festival, but Plinius never knows when to stop his research or, come to that, his speeches. He just *had* to tell us about the history books he'd unearthed on his latest expedition.

You must understand this about Plinius: his father named him after Pliny the Old, hoping to make him into the insufferable know-it-all he has become. I, on the other hand, changed my given name for that of Apicius, the gastronome of the Empire. I'm an epicure to Plinius' stoic. He feels I've lost the essence of the Roman Ideal. I know I'm its purest form.

To Plinius, the Ideal is a Hadrian's Wall of accumulated facts, merely a barricade against another Total War. If anything, he self-identifies with the early days of the Republic: military discipline and plain lentil soup. He fails to grasp the majesty and grandeur of the Empire. Plinius will never understand that fruit is at its sweetest just as it's beginning to rot.

Plinius despises me, of course, and being much older than me and having an elevated position in the city's hierarchy, feels compelled to tell me all he thinks is wrong about my behavior. I would happily ignore his lecturing if he didn't keep pointing out anachronisms in my garments. I don't care if my sandals are three hundred years too old for the clasp on my cape, if this makes the ensemble more aesthetically pleasing!

The books Plinius discovered in the abandoned cities, and which he's so eager to tell us about, indicate that Roman statues were not the elegant white marble we've always known and admired. Instead they may have been painted in the gaudiest of colors. Plinius shows us pictures of how old historians from before the Total Wars imagined the painted statues—childish renderings, mocking the nobility of the Roman Ideal. An insult! Does Plinius, among all people, not see how wrong this is? You can't ask people to adhere to an Ideal and then keep tweaking it.

And then he goes and does it. He cites the "eksray machines" those ancient historians used to seek defamatory evidence. This causes much muttering in the audience, mainly coming from those factions that would love an excuse to overthrow the Governor and take his place. A level of finesse clearly beyond Plinius' grasp.

"Enough!" the Governor intervenes, seeking to reign in Plinius before his second-in-command strays too far. After all, when our Governor took his position he changed his name to Augustus, who ruled the Empire for over forty years, and he can't do so without Plinius. As tiresome as he can sometimes be, Plinius is the only one who knows how everything in the city works. "Have you forgotten why our ancestors went back to the Roman Ideal?"

"Of course not, Governor," replies Plinius, raising his chin. "You know I only seek to better understand the Roman times so that we can adhere more closely to their purest form. I would never dream of trying to understand the machinery itself!" Plinius turns to face the assembly. "I'm only too aware that any level of technology beyond the Roman Ideal would inevitably lead us to industry, and then rapidly to another Total War. No one works harder than me to prevent this from happening."

"If I may, my dear Governor," says Octavius, using his most unctuous voice. "I'm sure none of us questions the good will of Plinius, but I think it's worth noting that his namesake died in the Vesuvius eruption, which he went to observe *out of scientific curiosity*. Is this really the man we want leading us?"

"My dear Octavius," Plinius cuts him off, smiling at Octavius' lack of subtlety in trying to instigate a feud between him and the Governor. "Augustus is our one and only leader, and I'm sure I have never strived to gain any influence beyond my position." Plinius runs his fingers through his white goatee as he glares at Octavius, a man so uneducated that he once pinned his toga with an Ottoman brooch. "Besides, we all understand that a namesake is never more than a namesake. An inspiration, not a template."

The Governor nods.

"All smoke bombs are in place for the closing ceremony." Plinius goes on, knowing it's the one thing we've come to hear. "My assistants and I will use the respite from regular activity to brew the next batches of the revealing draught."

There's a murmur of approval in the room, and a couple of guffaws from the more excitable members of our assembly. Hardly the sophisticated behavior one would expect from a patrician, but who can blame them? In their month of unrestricted freedom our slaves provide us with the thrill of being fully alive. An unrivalled glee that makes our bodies vibrate like the taut strings on a lyre, for who can be content with merely existing, when death itself may be waiting for you to get back home?

"Then we shall meet at dusk in front of the Temple for the inaugural procession," says the Governor, concluding the assembly.

Now the Vanishing Festival is about to begin, we all feel inclined to look more kindly on Plinius' transgressions. The dear old fool! The man is so obsessed with facts he's even taught his Cheshire slaves to read, so they can recite to him as he takes his daily cold bath. One would think this kind of abuse would get Plinius killed during the Festival, but he has never showed up with his throat cut by a kitchen knife, or as Gratianus the merchant, sitting under a cypress tree with his eyes gouged out.

More than that, Plinius' Cheshires have never even bothered to run away. If it wasn't for the trouble they'd cause to their master, I believe that his Cheshires would be happy to remain fully visible throughout the Festival, and not join in their peers' revelling.

How it must irk Plinius that I, out of all our fellow citizens, am the only other patrician to enjoy a similar level of devotion from my Cheshire slaves! In my case, admittedly, because after I've had the *foie* from a fig-fed goose I have no use for the rest of the animal, and not having my ingrained desire for personal beauty, my household

Cheshires have become pot-bellied instead of the usual skin-and-bones. Unlike the rest of Cheshires in the city, they can often be heard laughing as they shoo the peacocks in the inner courtyard.

We all leave the assembly and go home to prepare. The streets had been decorated the night before by an army of Cheshire slaves impatiently nudging us towards the Vanishing Festival. The Cheshires have made the city into a gigantic ossuary. Wind chimes made of white-painted canes like tibias and ribs, and garlands of teeth-like white corn hang across the streets. Even the Temple's columns have been covered in skeletal decorations.

The Vanishing Festival has always been my favorite time of the year. I'll grant that not enjoying the Cheshires' services for a month is inconvenient, but if I can manage two full-blown banquets during each Festival, any regular household should be able to function without much trouble.

During the Festival a maid may lay with as many men as she pleases and still get married as a virgin. A man can grant his favors to other men and not be thought any the less for it. The citizens dance, drink, laugh hysterically, run naked on the streets, play pranks on each other, scream at the top of their lungs. Fortunes are gambled away joyously, for there may not be time left to spend them. Honey-wine and mead run as abundant as rainwater in spring, and mountains of food are devoured. Not all of them delicacies, I agree, but then I can only vouch for what is served on my table.

As much as I delight in the flamingo tongues and amphorae of fish sauce described by my namesake in his *De Re Coquinaria,* I have of course adapted the ancient recipes. So many animals and plants have become extinct between Roman times and ours, and yet so many others have been discovered beyond the confines of the old Empire! I feast on chocolate-covered quail, curry-laced apricot marmalade and sake-marinated oysters.

I run home to check everything is ready for my famous first night banquet, and prepare for the parade. My Cheshires left the food on the tables before dawn, and arranged the red draperies on the walls so the focus will be on the table decorations and the new floor mosaic. I'll only have to light the lamps and the braziers once I get back home.

But first I need to put on my finery for the parade. Nothing too subtle, nothing too garish. I don't want to look like one of those churlish merchants who put on fake armor and decorate their unblemished helmets with eagle feathers, or cover themselves in wolf and leopard pelts, as if they've just returned from an arduous campaign in some imaginary colony.

I arrive at the Temple in time for Augustus' inaugural speech, and the procession down the Temple's stairs and along the Cardo Maximus. Two standard bearers flank our Governor as we march to the sound of cymbals, drums, trumpets and horns. The torches that line the streets reflect on golden brooches and burnished leather epaulettes, on the emeralds and rubies embedded in tiaras and rings.

Only Plinius and his family—his haughty wife Livia and his beautiful and proud daughter Aemilia—aren't wearing any jewels, if only because they wear austerity as a crown. Poor Aemilia, named by Plinius after a vestal virgin! If only she was a man, she could change her name without permission from her father or a future husband.

The rest of us parade in our full regalia under a baldachin of make-believe teeth that smile down at us, as we synchronize our steps to the beat of the tympana drum, and pretend the Vanishing Festival is ours to control.

Then the true procession starts. A silent river of marching skeletons, separating into smaller strands as it is too mighty to fit in the Cardo Maximus. The Cheshires are at their weakest during the parade and move slowly and ungainly under the swaying garlands. Their silent procession is much less ordered, but much more solemn than ours. After eleven months of enforced visibility they get to reveal their true nature, although their rib-cages and grins and eye-sockets, and every indentation on their skulls, are still perfectly visible.

In the following weeks, as they recover their strength, we'll see isolated groups of Cheshires as slowly vanishing skeletons, dancing on the streets to the sound of the cane wind chimes. Or splashing in a green pond, not minding the loud protests of the ducks; chasing each other atop the city walls; or standing on each other's shoulders to reach the tallest branches of an orange tree, while the orchard's owner pretends not to see them.

They'll become much more energetic as the days go by and their bones become translucent—weakness being a side effect of the revealing draught they must take daily—but the inaugural procession is the one time us citizens realize how vastly outnumbered we are.

As much as Plinius insists that the Festival restores equilibrium to the city, he's too much of a romantic to admit the Festival's true goal: to prevent our slaves from dying and let them get their strength back, so they can carry on with their duties for another year. Not that I'm complaining about the Festival, quite the opposite!

Although thirty days is not enough for the draught's effects to completely wear off on most Cheshires, and they'll remain visible at least as a grin suspended mid-air, often with a few vertebrae attached. Each year a handful of Cheshires will become fully invisible well before the end of the Festival, and then—*Oh, joy!*—the fun will begin.

Will the invisible Cheshire stay put and wait out the

Festival? Will she climb the city walls and escape into the desert, or maybe to the cities with infinite buildings, where the bombs from the Total Wars still make you sick? Or will he go on a rampage before running away, and avenge any real or imaginary wrongs?

Plinius assures us that on his expeditions to the abandoned cities he's encountered many a runaway Cheshire. They take advantage of their invisibility to throw rocks at him, and on his last trip, steal his horses (which really unnerved Plinius, and Manius and I found hilarious).

At the end of each Festival the city will contain a few less Cheshires and a few (or many) less citizens. Some may not have died at the hands of an invisible servant. Every year a couple of patricians drunkenly fall into their own piscinas and drown.

As the smoke bombs are set off and coat the city and its inhabitants in a soot-black patina that will take weeks for the Cheshires to completely scrub off from walls and paving stones, the rest of us will be hung over and fatter, and spent from too much lovemaking, and our purses will be empty and our feet will hurt from dancing. But we'll be exhilarated for having survived, and never embarrassed—not even for our most outrageous deeds—for we have lived to see the end of yet another Festival.

Some will vouch to treat their Cheshires better the following year, but our memory is short and our nature relentless, and thus the Festival will never lose its thrill.

I hurry back home after the parade. I don't want the guests to have to wait, and I need some time for the braziers to warm up the triclinium. The warmth will bring out the scent of the new sandalwood recliners, and will make my guests comfortable in any level of disrobement they may choose. Propriety will be shed tonight like a carapace we've outgrown, and although parties will grow wilder as the Festival progresses, it's not unlikely that a few of my younger guests will want to display their bejeweled bodies.

I give a last look at the room before opening the front door to welcome my guests. I've outshone myself with the table's centerpiece, if I say so myself. Three stag heads facing out, their antlers casting flickering shadows on the walls. The stags' pelts have been kept on, and their eyes have been closed to preserve an illusion of peacefulness. The heads have been slowly cooked in a steam oven of my own design, so that the most daring among my guests may delight in the warm contents of the animals' crowned heads.

The stags are what initially inspired me to make the whole feast revolve around a woodland theme. There are also quails in truffle sauce, yellow foot mushrooms, mountains of fresh berries, boar marinated in wine infused with rosemary and thyme, and six chestnut-stuffed pheasants, with a mixture of crushed nuts and cardamom that my most small-handed Cheshire patiently introduced between the birds' skins and their meat before roasting them whole. I can't see how my guests could fail to be impressed.

I wake up on the hard mosaic floor. My head pounds. I look at the mess around me. There are metal jugs and pieces of broken pottery on the floor. At least the guests are all gone, the Gods be praised! The braziers must have died out hours ago, and the air and the floor are both terribly cold, although I'm always one of the few members on any banquet to remain fully clothed. All the bones in my body ache, and as I sit up, my head spins and I feel a strong urge to throw up that I manage to overcome. I groan. Plinius speaks of the Vanishing Festival as a penitence, and I believe he must refer to hosts having to clean up themselves after a banquet, a thought that fills *me* with dread, too.

Flashes of the banquet come to me. Truffle sauce running down Pythia's neck as she gorged herself on quail. Manius overturning a mulled wine jar and the red liquid spreading on the mosaic floor. Cackling laughter as a very drunk and naked young man—can't remember who, exactly—ran across the room with a stag's antlers on his head, pretending to chase Flavia, who ran away giggling. A voice whispering in my ear:

"Forget Octavius, he's being used and is too foolish to realize it. Someone else in the assembly will make a grab for the Governor's position. You just wait."

Rumors. Gossip. Mindless fun and carefully crafted jabs. All in all, quite a successful party.

The fun continues over the following days. I'm invited to many banquets and parties all over the city. Sometimes I feel I must refuse, as I'm quite certain the host is only trying to get invited in return, or I simply don't want to inflict such pain on my palate.

It rains for three days in a row, which only keeps me home during the light hours. Some of the white-painted canes suffer water damage and are replaced. The Cheshires have always been fiercely proud of their skeletal decorations.

Every day I put out a platter with cold meats, some bread and a couple of oranges in the courtyard for my Cheshires, like you are supposed to do. I often see them there, teasing the peacocks. The birds circle their fading skeletons as if appraising a threat, and then jump at their chests claws-first, amidst the Cheshires' laughter. My Cheshires didn't use to be this cheeky, but I guess not having them run away during the Festival also means they're getting more comfortable with every passing year.

No one in the city questions the Cheshires' obligation

to pay for their ancestors' crimes by serving as our slaves, although some of us go about it more gently than others. True, the Cheshires' ability to become invisible at will was used by all five sides on the Total Wars. But it was our side that discovered the revealing draught, which gave the Cheshires their new name and position.

Before that, we only had the smoke bombs to unmask any invisible soldiers, and they certainly weren't as effective as the draught! After we invented the draught and annihilated our enemies, the Total Wars were over. Doesn't that give us the victor's right to rule undisputed?

Alas, my Cheshires seem to be forgetting their place. I go back inside to pick my clothes for the Governor's mid-Festival banquet. It's all I can do to pretend not to notice their disgraceful treatment of the peacocks.

Everybody who's anybody attends the Governor's dinner. This banquet is always carefully timed so that the town gossips have the first inklings on whose Cheshires may make it to full invisibility, and who in those housings is more deserving of a comeuppance, without any actual deaths having taken place yet.

Augustus' banquets are by necessity more formal than most, but he makes up for it by adding an extra layer of extravagance. This year two huge cages containing cheetahs flank the entrance. I must admit that I'm slightly jealous. One of the things that first attracted me to my namesake was that after Apicius squandered his inheritance in luxurious delicacies, rather than accept a modest life, he poisoned himself. I find that the epitome of elegance. What better ending to a life, than the one you choose and administer? And yet, despite how much I spend on my banquets, I've always stopped short of total bankruptcy. That Augustus' caged cheetahs are well beyond my grasp, or my daring, seems like a failing on my side.

Although Plinius would probably prefer to stay away with his assistants and work on the revealing draught, even he can't afford to miss his boss' banquet. His wife and daughter join him, if only to look down on the other guests. Beautiful Aemilia is looking particularly pale and withdrawn. I wonder if Plinius forces her to remain indoors for the duration of the Festival, poor thing.

She catches me looking at her. I smile. She frowns. Everything's normal, then.

"We underestimate the Cheshires at our own risk!" I hear Plinius berating Octavius.

Plinius is so red-faced and agitated that for an instant I wonder if he's drunk, and I tell myself I must remember to tell Flavia, it'll be such a laugh! But then he becomes his old self and adds:

"The Roman Ideal is a discipline, not an excuse to gorge ourselves and drink till we pass out. All this self-indulgence will be our downfall."

Sometimes I think Plinius would have us believe he was breastfed by a she-wolf, if he could get away with it! But I lie. Plinius is too honest for that, and besides, he lacks the imagination. At any rate, he's managed to squash the fun out of the evening.

Augustus' food is good but uninspired, and I'm so bored by the formal chatter that I leave early. As I walk back home through the decorated alleys, white-painted canes strike one another in the breeze, making a song like peals of laughter. I recognize the ginger cat in front of my friend Manius' house. I know for a fact that the cat's an excellent mouser and a fellow lover of lamb kidneys, so I feel compelled to stop and pat it.

"Hi, there," I say as I kneel next to the animal. "Shouldn't you be guarding the pantry against the mice hordes?"

The cat meows. It turns towards me, and I see fur on its side bending unnaturally as the animal rubs against what it must perceive as a man-shaped smell.

A chill runs down my spine.

I stand up.

"Sorry," I mutter, and I leave as fast as I can. It's all I can do to not break into a run.

Was the Cheshire following me? Was he waiting for Manius instead, or did he just stop for the cat as I did? Isn't it too early in the Festival for him to be fully invisible already?

I'm covered in cold sweat and I'm starting to shiver, even as my legs and lungs burn. There's a considerable distance between Manius' house and mine, and I must reach it before an invisible hand grabs my shoulder. Or stabs my back. I consider barricading the doors when I get home, but then I realize he's got five accomplices inside my house.

I don't leave the house for the next four days and refuse to receive any visitors. It rains again, and I spend a whole afternoon wrapped in blankets, watching the rain as it falls through the opening on the atrium's ceiling into the impluvium. I'm petrified. I can't do anything about my own Cheshires, who come and go as they please.

I can sometimes count five skulls out in the courtyard, so it would seem that the fully invisible Cheshire I met on the street wasn't mine. Unless, and I can't believe this never occurred to me before, that during the Festival it would be as easy for the Cheshires to visit each other's houses as it is for us, and therefore some of the Cheshires in the house may not be mine. Surely I've always been a kind master?

I spend night and day debating whether I should warn Manius, but I don't even know if the Cheshire I met is his, or if he bears any ill will towards his master. I don't even know if he's a he, beyond a feeling of physical bulk that may be just in my mind.

By its third week, the Festival is always in full swing and any remaining concerns about propriety have been cast aside. For the first time in my life, I don't want anything to do with it.

As strange as it may seem for a social creature such as me, the truth is I don't have many close friends. Not even a handful. I was raised by an elderly uncle after my parents died. If I have ever opened up to anyone it has always been to the most warm-hearted of my fellows, and therefore I always assumed that anyone made nervous by the Festival had what was coming to them.

To think I laughed at Gratianus, sitting against a wall and throwing breadcrumbs to surround himself with sparrows! He hoped their flight would alert him of his murderer's arrival. We all knew how Gratianus treated his Cheshires, but still, I shouldn't have laughed.

As days go by, I convince myself that if the Cheshire I encountered bore any ill will towards Manius or myself, we'd be dead already. It must have been a simple coincidence. Silly me, scared out of my wits by a Cheshire petting a kitty!

I'm in half-mind to suspend my second banquet, but I dread thinking what people would make of it. I'm home one evening, trying out different arrangements for the triclinium's furniture, when there's a knock at the door.

"Aemilia?" I'm shocked to see Plinius' daughter at my door.

She says nothing and comes into the vestibulum. I follow her, perplexed.

"Are we alone?" she asks when we reach the dining hall. I think I can smell spirits on her breath, but that's just not possible.

"Your guess is as good as mine. I mean... yes, I think my Cheshires' skulls are still quite visible, if that's what you mean."

"Well, my cousin's Cheshire is not," she says, as if the revelation should make me shudder.

And then I understand.

"What did you do, Aemilia?"

"I stole a pair of sapphire earrings from my cousin Quintina, and I told everyone I'd seen her maid trying them on," Aemilia lowers her eyes, but I can't tell if it's remorse she feels, or shame that I know she's never been as pure as she likes to pretend. "My uncle beat her really hard, and now she can't be seen," she adds, and looks back at me, defiantly.

"How do you even know which one of your uncle's Cheshires she is?"

"Oh, I know. She lost her front teeth during the beating. Her ugly mouth has been chasing me for the last week, just to let me know she was almost invisible already, and I haven't seen her for a couple of days."

"I still don't understand. What can I do to help you?"

"You?" Aemilia laughs. "What could you possibly do?"

There's shock in her eyes that I would think myself so important. She continues to laugh, but I forgive her, for I hear the beginning of hysteria in her voice.

"There's only one person in the city powerful enough to help me, and that's my father," she stares into my eyes, to prove that she still is and will always be above me. "But he refused to set the smoke bombs early and end the Festival so that his daughter may live. Says the city's bigger than him or his family. Says I should never have taken those earrings and blamed an innocent." She chuckles bitterly. "My father loves Cheshires so much it's disgusting. If I'd ever stolen from my mother, he'd have believed our Cheshires before me."

"I still don't see what this has to do with me."

As a reply, Aemilia swiftly removes her garments and stands naked in front of me.

"I shall give you my body to do anything you want with it, on the condition that afterward you must go and tell my father. Isn't this what you've always wanted?"

"No," I mutter under my breath. "Not really." But I don't think she hears me.

Aemilia has come to my house to be defiled, and I don't see how I could get out of it and keep my pride. I try to guess what weirdness or deviancy she expects from me. I have her lay on the long table, and get a jar of honey with cinnamon and clover I'd prepared for the banquet, and pour it all over her. I lick it off her skin as she tells me all the nasty things her father has ever said about me, some of which I've heard before, some of which may be true or she may be making them up: That is people like me that will bring the city down. That I'm a good-for-nothing, lazy, spineless buffoon. That the few friends I have are complete idiots, or only after my money...

"Out!" I cut her off, getting away from her and pointing at the door.

She raises her head from the table as if she doesn't understand why I've stopped.

"Out of my house!" I scream. "Your father raised a common thief. Neither of you are fit to criticize me!" I say, hating the quaver in my voice.

She's still not moving and there's half a smirk on her lips, so I grab the empty honey jar and throw it against the back wall, as far from both of us as possible. I see her flinch and at last she seems to get the message. She jumps off the table, grabs her discarded clothes and leaves the room. A few moments later, I hear the front door close. Presumably

Aemilia has left my house fully clothed, even if still covered in honey. She probably thinks it only makes her look more regal.

The following morning my neighbor tells me Aemilia's body has been found in an alley behind the Forum. She appears to have been hit on the back of the head. Her expression was peaceful, so the general opinion is that her teeth were bashed in after she was dead, which is a mercy.

It takes me a couple of days to pull myself together.

Even if I expected it, Aemilia's demise has rattled me, although now that she's dead I feel no obligation to tell her father about her visit.

I'm forcing myself to focus on my second banquet's preparations. This late into the Festival meals must be fully eked out of preserves, which is always a challenge. Not that I don't do a good job of it. My cod with dates, peanuts and saffron was a huge success last year.

I'm buying sage and cumin at one of my favorite spice dealers. Many customers show signs of inebriation, even this early in the morning. I've been uncharacteristically sober for most of the Festival, and this has soured my disposition towards more enthusiastic revelers. I chide myself. I mustn't become a grumpy old man.

As I'm smelling a handful of cumin, Domitius comes running into the shop.

"They've found Plinius floating on the canal!" he shouts.

I feel the blood drain from my face. I hear moaning, and some barely contained chuckles.

"Aemilia," someone mutters.

My head spins. Words boil around me. No one believes that Plinius' Cheshires would ever harm him, so they attribute his death to grief over Aemilia's passing.

I know otherwise.

Plinius knew what was coming, and besides, suicide wasn't his style. It was one of us that killed Plinius. A patrician. The knowledge chokes me like a noose. I feel faint. I lose my balance, and as I try to steady myself I knock over a black pepper sack. The grains spill all over the shop's floor like an eruption of black lava. Cackling laughter stabs my ears. I run away.

It's only a couple of streets to my house, but I'm not sure I can make it. My legs barely support me, they threaten to give way at every stride. The teeth-like garlands sway in the breeze, taunting me. I can barely see the street. I can't stop crying.

As I stumble through my front door, I fall on the hard mosaic floor and hit my knees. I moan in pain. I hear laughter and see a jaw floating mid-air not ten feet from me, opening and closing along with the barking laughs. My heart tightens into a fist, but the Cheshire doesn't get any closer. Not to strike me. Not to help me, either. He just stands there as I limp towards my rooms pretending not to see him, although I can hear him chuckling clearly enough. He must think I'm drunk, I tell myself.

Once inside my rooms I cover my face with my hands and weep. My chest heaves as I sob uncontrollably. I could pretend that I'm weeping for Plinius, but what would be the use? I weep for me. I weep in fear. Now that I sense turmoil ahead of us, I realize that I'll never find the courage to end my life before it's too late. Instead, I'll cling to it with the desperate determination of cowards.

Someone murdered Plinius to take him out of the way. An unseen menace within the assembly that will strike Augustus before long. And then what? Plinius and Augustus were never my friends, but they didn't need to be. They always put the city and its safety before anything else, and I can't imagine that whoever takes their place will do the same. Maybe the new ruler will use the Cheshires against the city, or he'll simply underestimate them. I'm afraid that we're living in the last days of the Roman Ideal. Do the Cheshires sense it, too?

The thought terrifies me.

What difference does it make, to be in the midst of a Total War or of a battle restricted to the confines of your city, if you can't escape it either way?

I hear the sound of pottery being shattered, followed by laughter.

It won't be long now.

Elmore Banks was a Bad Man and His Gun Had a Name and Her Name was Celia

Alexander Stanmyer

ELMORE BANKS was a bad man and his gun had a name and her name was Celia.

But now Celia was missing and Banks was missing teeth and fluid leaked from his broken skull and into his eyes and the Dakota sun was too damned hot.

Flies buzzed a symphony.

Banks was a gunslinger and a card player and the toughest motherfucker in these parts.

But Celia was missing and what was a gunslinger without his gun but a coward who can raise his hand quicker than the other cowards?

Plumes of blue smoke rose from their cigarettes and pipes and cigars like strands of cosmic dust. The pianist played something sad. Some Austrian dirge. The hour for cabaret had long since passed. Rain pattered against thin glass windows. Piles of ivory chips rose from the felt tabletop like stalagmites of yellowing bone. Whiskey glasses cluttered the table like standing stones.

Banks was black and the rest of the men were white and Banks was winning and all in the bar were aware of this fact.

Five card stud was the game. Banks had been dealt a face-up hand of black aces and eights. He would have laughed at the portent of that but for the fact that there was near close to three thousand dollars in the pot.

His card in the hole was the ace of hearts and he had slipped there himself and with it he held the nuts. Banks pushed the rest of his chips into the pot. All but one folded.

One man, a ruddy Scotsman by the name of Silas, called Banks' bet. Banks hadn't liked the man from the start. He seemed uncomfortable in his own skin. His teeth were rotting and his breath stank. His eyes shined with hate for Banks, and while being hated by a white man wasn't a new development, it never got any easier to deal with.

Banks flipped his card and locked eyes with Silas and the bar went silent.

"That was your deal." Silas' eyes were bloodshot. His cheeks were flush with cheap whiskey. He had held a full house of kings over sixes.

Banks raked the chips towards him. "It was."

"Fuck you then." Silas pointed a finger at the gunslinger. Stared him down for some time, a stare which Banks held. "I'll be seeing you soon." He stumbled off from the table and out into the night and rain. He muttered as he went and Banks caught the words mother and wife and money.

"He got a gun?" Banks asked the room.

"A Griswold he won off of some Reb from Kentucky. Likes to show it off when he ain't playing cards," the bartender said.

"Well," Banks said. "I'd recommend one of you go convince Silas not to do anything stupid." Banks pulled back his coat and tapped the dark, wooden grip of Celia. Her iron shone like death in the lamplight.

"You the one I heard about?" one of the other players asked. He was an old man with brown teeth and white hair and a pipe that hadn't once left his teeth since he entered the bar nearly twelve hours earlier. "So fast they say you made a deal with the devil?"

"Might just be," Banks said. "Ain't been beat yet."

The old man nodded. "Say Johnny," he called to the bartender. "If you don't want Silas' blood on these boards, best send someone to cool his temper."

Johnny sent a pair of his barboys out after Silas.

"Thanks, old timer," Banks said.

The man winked at Banks in a way that he found unsettling. Another hand was dealt.

As agreed upon, the game continued until sunup. Banks won more hands. Lost some, too. Came out a richer man regardless. Silas did not return to the bar.

Banks ambled back to the boarding house in the grey dawn light. In his room was a whore named Ella. She was half white and half Indian and Banks had paid for a week's worth of her company. He liked her figure. Upon bringing her to his room, he had told Ella that there were to be two rules. One, that she never touch Celia. Two, that she never ask about the woman for whom the gun was so anointed.

Banks counted bills and stashed them in a lockbox beneath the bed. They shared a bottle of dark, red wine and then they fucked. She fell asleep snoring softly on his chest. Banks stared up at the ceiling. Kept replaying that hand over and over again in his head. Smiled at just how damned fast he was. That fifth ace, slid right in. None of those hillbilly peckerwoods the wiser.

After some time, he slept.

Celia was missing and Banks was in a ditch.

The limbs of trees were like bones and he could see black fungus clinging to their undersides.

Funny, he thought, how a man can go his whole life and miss ever noticing such things.

Funny, he thought, how a man's brain can ooze from his skull and he think such things in his final moments.

One of Silas' brood made a move on Banks in the streets the day following the poker game. Banks was on his way to the bank and saw the kid from the corner of his eye.

The kid carried a shotgun beneath his coat. He was slow on the draw.

Banks was not.

Celia jumped in Banks' hand and made her beautiful music. A bullet carved a trench through the boy's skull and brain and bone splattered against the saloon's wall. The shotgun's barrel hadn't made it more than a few inches in the air. The kid's left leg twitched and sent puffs of dust into the air.

"He drew on me first," Banks said to the smattering of people gathered on the thoroughfare. "You all seen it."

Someone called for the sheriff. They were white and the boy Banks killed was white and Banks was black. The arithmetic was easy.

Banks hadn't met the sheriff in town yet. If he was a racist sonofabitch, then Banks might as well start tying his own noose. If he wasn't, then he figured he better start making plans to leave town regardless.

Either way, to leave the scene might as well be an admission of guilt.

He holstered Celia. Licked dry lips and eyed the townsfolk. He was twitchy. One man scratched his ass and Banks nearly skinned Celia a second time.

Banks studied the boy's remains. There was something about the scene that bothered him. Banks had killed plenty of men before. Had seen death in the war and on the streets of the West.

It was the boy's blood, Banks realized.

Too thick, too dark. Closer to black than crimson. It ran slowly down the saloon's wall. Molasses-like, Banks thought. And the chunks of brain and flesh... they quivered. Ever so slightly. Banks wiped sweat from his brow and wondered if Emma hadn't slipped laudanum in his morning coffee.

The sheriff showed a few moments later.

He wore a suit and an ascot and he smelled of beer and he carried a Winchester. He wore a tarnished star and it glinted dully in the sun. Banks tipped his hat to the man.

"You kill that boy?" the sheriff asked.

Banks nodded.

"You draw first? Or him?"

"He did."

"Now why would he do such a thing?"

"Beat his buddy Silas in stud. Took him for near three thousand dollars. I suspect that's why."

The sheriff's face turned sour at Silas' name. He nodded and spat on the dusty thoroughfare. He turned to the few that had lingered since the shooting. "That true? The boy drew first?"

They looked at each other. One woman shrugged. "That's the truth of it sheriff."

"Boy couldn't have been older than fourteen." The sheriff kicked at the dirt. He sighed. "You leave town by sundown tomorrow. Otherwise, you hang."

"Fair enough," Banks said.

Banks withdrew what money he had deposited in the bank, bought a bottle of red wine and a bottle of white and a week's worth of trail provisions, and spent the rest of the day dozing in Ella's arms. Night came and they got drunk. They ordered steaks from the kitchen downstairs. The stars shivered outside and Banks thought of the nights he had spent bivouacked during the war.

Banks had Emma read a dime novel to him aloud like Celia used to.

Eventually they slept.

In the morning, Banks woke up to the smell of blood and shit.

In the pulps they never tell you about how people shit themselves when they die.

Emma was dead, her throat slit. Her blood was all over the bed. Stuck to her forehead were four playing cards: black aces and eights.

Banks kept expecting to wake up.

When the hangover kicked in, he figured he wasn't dreaming.

Banks cracked the door to his room and called down to the man who worked the desk downstairs.

"Yessir?" The man responded.

"Draw me a bucket of warm water. Bring a brush and rags. Soap if you've got it. Leave it outside my door."

"Anything else? Breakfast, maybe?"

"Whiskey," Banks called back.

An hour later and Banks had scrubbed what blood he could from himself. He draped a blanket over Emma and stuffed her corpse beneath the bed. He put on his duster and gun belt. Wore a knife in his boot, too—a thin, wicked thing he had won in a poker game in Deadwood. A knife for killing. Banks stuffed his winnings at the bottom of his rucksack.

Banks locked the door to the boarding room behind him as he went.

He took the bottle of bourbon with him.

When Banks opened the door to the livery, the old timer from the poker game was standing there.

His pipe was still in his mouth. Next to him stood a woman. She wore an old, ill-fitting dress that was stained darkly in places.

He cradled a Henry in his arms and it was pointed at Banks' chest. The man's finger curled around the trigger.

"Guess I ain't leaving," Banks said.

"Nope," the man said. "You ain't."

Banks right hand twitched. Celia called to him.

"I wouldn't," the old man said. "Lest' you want a bullet in your chest. Put down the bottle and take off your iron. Nice and slow."

Banks set the bottle on the floor and undid his gun belt and tossed it at the feet of the old man. "Sorry, girl," he said.

The man kicked the gun across the room and Banks winced as Celia spun away. "Now be a good colored boy and turn around," the old man said.

The woman tied a length of rope tightly around Banks' wrists while the old man kept the rifle trained on Banks' head. Then the man emptied Celia and her cartridges clattered to floor. He stuffed her into his coat pocket. He went through Banks' rucksack until he found the cash layered at the bottom and then he nodded and slung the bag onto his back.

"Here's what's going to happen," the man said. "We're going to walk out of town. You're going to be quiet about it. We are going to meet Silas sometime this afternoon. Then, he's going to educate you about the way of the universe.

"Then we'll give you to her.

"And she'll take you, and change you, and you won't be you no more. And there will be pain regardless of the outcome.

"Got it?"

"Fuck you," Banks said.

———————

They left the livery through the back door and slipped out of town and into the woods and hills. The man kept his rifle aimed at Bank's back as they walked. If anyone in town noticed their departure, they did not make a fuss. The rope was tied tightly around Bank's wrist and his hands at first ached and then went numb.

The man directed Banks to a rough trail that led up and into the woods. Pine crowded in so thickly that their needles seemed closer to black in the dimness. They walked until the sun began to sink towards the horizon.

They stopped in a small glade. Silas sat under a tree at the edge of the glen with a book open in front of him. In the center of the glen rose a standing stone easily as large as Banks.

The stone was as black as pitch and Bank's gaze was drawn to it as an alcoholic's is to drink. Banks was transfixed. His mouth filled with saliva and his stomach roiled. His cock grew hard and he had an urge to get on his hands in knees and dig in the earth and find out what that stone marked. To dig and dig until skin peeled from his fingers and his nails peeled away and to dig still.

"Thanks for fetching him, Uncle Bill." Silas closed his book and rose to his feet.

Banks snapped out of his trance. His head ached.

"Was nothing, Silas. You know I'd do anything for you. Anything for her." Bill handed Celia over to Silas who stuffed it into the waist of his paints as if she were some trophy.

Banks found the old man's fawning over the youth off putting in a way he couldn't quite figure. It wasn't just that Silas was younger, though that was part of it. It was the earnestness that struck Banks as wrong. As if the old man worshipped the young one.

The woman sauntered up to Silas and he gave her a peck on the cheek. "Go on up to the house now and get dinner started," he told her. She nodded and followed a trail out on the other side of the Glen.

"You know." Silas turned and faced Banks. "That was one of my children that you shot today. We were just going to bushwhack you and take your greenbacks. But now, now we're short a worker."

"Boy drew on me," Banks said. "Didn't have a choice."

Silas smiled. His teeth were as brown as dirt. "I have many, many more children." His breath stank.

"How'd you get into my room? The door was locked."

"We can slip between the cracks of the world," Silas said. "You'll be able to soon as well. With the right persuasion, flesh and bone can become so very malleable. Let's go meet my Motherwife."

———•·•———

Banks was in a ditch and he was dying.

He turned his body and everything hurt. His *insides* hurt.

There was something next to him. The boy whose head he had grooved in town, except his head was whole now.

Mostly.

The boy's skin was... unbuttoned down the front. An

outer shell of skin and flesh remained. The boy's insides were gone as if someone had scooped him out like one might do to a melon.

Banks noticed then that there were more like the boy in the ditch. A dozen more? Two? It was hard to say. Some were covered with leaves and pine needles and dirt and some were furred white and black with fungus and mold. Flies swarmed.

Silas' home loomed on the hillside above.

Banks groaned and wished for Celia and a quicker end to this nightmare.

———•—•—•———

Silas lived in what Banks supposed you'd have to call a mansion. The house was big enough for the name, at least. A monster up on the hill above the glen. It was ramshackle and sprawling in its construction. It was a tumorous thing that bulged with errant rooms and floors and turrets that had been added here and there without any thought to aesthetic or stability.

"You know how I built this?" Silas asked as they climbed the gentle hill that lead up to the front door.

"Slaves."

"Ain't you a smart Negro? Though I prefer the terms servants to slaves."

"Servants?" Banks scoffed. "Call it what it is. Slavery. How else would an inbred shit heel like you get a house so big?"

Silas kicked in the back of Banks' knee and the man went down to the ground. "Be respectful now," he said. "I got knives, I got rope. She needs you alive to take you, that's true. But she don't need you whole. I'd start, I think, with your shooting fingers."

Banks grit his teeth and said nothing. He'd need those fingers, were he to have a chance to escape this nightmare.

They went inside and found themselves in the parlor. Heavy shades were drawn over the windows. A dozen or so people were spread out through the dark room. Some young, some old, some men, and some women. Some sat on furniture, others on the floor, some leaned against the walls, and others just stood there still as oaks. They all turned their heads to look at Banks.

"Say hello to your soon to be brother," Silas said.

"Hello," they spoke in unison and their voices were cracked, dusty things. As if they weren't used to speaking, as if they didn't have much use for words.

"I'll be right back," Silas said. "Uncle Bill. Make sure our guest doesn't go anywhere."

Bill pointed his rifle at Banks. Chewed on the end of his pipe.

Silas reappeared with a magic lantern and a chair and a box of slides. Celia, Banks noticed, was no longer tucked into the man's pants. Silas put the chair facing one bare wall and gestured for Banks to sit. Banks did, feeling the eyes of the others track his every movement.

Silas set up the lantern on an end table and pointed it at the wall.

"These slides are from Scotland, mostly. That's where my daddy was from. He's still there. Doing work, making preparations. Gathering resources. Money, connections, power.

"Anyways, my daddy was an entomologist. You know what that is, boy?"

"I'm sure you're aiming to tell me."

"A man who studies insects. An academic. Daddy's area of study was the metamorphosis of butterflies. In the archives of Edinburgh Castle, he found an old text called *Mutatis* written in Latin by a Roman Legionnaire and occultist stationed in Britannia. It was this book that led him to the first location of *them.* " Silas lit the kerosene lamp and inserted a slide into the lantern. The image of a cocoon hanging from a branch was projected upon the wall. The other figures in the room stared wordlessly at the image.

"Now, you might be wondering why I'm showing you this. It's because I want you to understand *exactly* what you'll be going through. It can be a difficult experience having one's insides melt, I know."

Banks thought of going for his knife and sticking it through the peckerwood's throat. His hands were tied, but he thought he still might have a chance at it. Bill would plug him, surely. But maybe he could take Silas out before he went. No, Banks decided, he planned on getting both of the bastards.

"After a caterpillar enters its cocoon, it devours itself. Turns itself into nothing more than a sac of ooze. Cut into that sac at the right time and caterpillar soup will leak out." Silas changed the slides. An image of a scalpel cutting into a cocoon shone on the wall. Green fluid oozed from it.

Silas continued, "Eventually, the soup reforms into something new, into a butterfly.

"You, boy, you will be undergoing your own metamorphosis.

"First, Motherwife, she'll put her spores in you. That's how it starts. They'll get in your throat and in your lungs and in your blood and brain. And even someone as quick on the draw as you are can't shoot away things you can't see."

Silas licked his lips. "And, just so you know, there's a little bit of *me* in her. So I'll be in you.

"After the spores are in you, the process starts. The spores will spread and multiply and fill you up. Your thoughts will get fuzzy. Your muscles will get weak. Your skin will harden and your insides will dissolve. Just like the pupa in its cocoon. It will, I'm afraid, hurt quite a lot. The soft parts go first: tongue, eyes, genitals, brain. Eventually, you will die.

"She'll reform the cooling meat into a new *you.* A better you. A more obedient you. Your skin will split and this new you will crawl out blinking into the sun and you will listen to her and you will listen to me and you will serve.

"Some of the old you will be in there, but you will no longer be human. Not really.

"You will be better."

"You are one crazy sonofabitch," Banks said.

Silas changed the slide. Banks found it hard to square what he was looking at. It was a photograph. A man crawled slick and wet and naked from a dead man's chest. The man on his knees wore the same face of the dead one.

"Beautiful, isn't it?" Silas said.

"That's not the word I would use."

"Let's go meet her."

They descended a set of spiral stairs that led deep into the earth. Silas carried a torch. Uncle Bill followed behind with his rifle. The rest of the brood stayed upstairs.

The stairs were steep and made out of wooden planks. Some were rotted through. At the bottom of the stairs was a tunnel that lead down and away from the house. They followed it a ways until it ended in a small room.

The room was hot, humid.

Instead of a wall of dirt or stone or brick was one of what could only be flesh. It was as pale as a cave fish and it pulsated and quivered and it was slick with something like sweat. Banks knew with a certainty that whatever being this was, he was only seeing a small bit of its massive form.

From the ceiling jutted the bottom of what Banks guessed was the standing stone in the glen.

Silas placed a hand on that wall of flesh. It quivered at his touch. He closed his eyes and moaned softly.

"Motherwife," he said, "I've missed you too,"

Banks head ached. His gorge rose. His patience, he decided, had reached its end.

"They're buried deep, all over the Earth—the one my daddy found beneath the moors was just the first," Silas said. "Waiting and waiting like insects in their cocoons. Like your American cicadas. Except instead of every seventeen years, their lifecycles are counted in the great epochs of the Earth.

"It's all cycles, boy. Everything. All of it. Cycles and circles. Birth and death and dreams and memories and even the stars.

"We came to America looking for more of them, for they will be waking soon. The megaliths, like the one you saw in the glade, they offer a powerful attraction, no?

"There's another in Kentucky. And another at the bottom of the Grand Canyon. My brother's up in New England. He wrote saying he found one in a place called Dunwich. They are elder beings, the motherwives. Not insects, but that's the closest comparison. Hierarchal hive-minds.

"We're different, us and them. As different as me and you. They're enlightened.

"It's the natural way of things.

"I've seen what they seen. And you will too.

"The universe is big and it's black and we're naught but puppets of flesh and muscle. They are the things that can traverse the cracks. They are knowing. They are *old.* They've ridden the winds of the stars and settled their spores throughout the cosmos. And they are *strong.* It's survival of the fittest. A man named Darwin said that. Not that you'd know much about him.

"Spencer."

"Huh?"

"Herbert Spencer said it. Not Darwin. Spencer was a racist asshole, just like you, Silas."

The wall parted slightly. Warm air rushed from it as if the thing exhaled. It smelled of fungus and rot and wet earth. Through that parted slit Banks saw only darkness and wet flesh. "Here she comes," Silas said.

The air grew thick, grew steamy, as if the room filled with a fine mist. Banks found it hard to breathe. The fetid smell worsened. Particles floated in the air.

"She's in you now," Silas said. He tittered.

Banks coughed. He reached a hand for his throat.

"She'll win your heart, fill your insides, spread her spore throughout your lungs. You'll die. Maybe glimpse that which lies beyond.

"Which, I'll tell you, is naught but darkness.

"But then she'll bring you back. Reform you. And the way you see things will change. You'll see the beauty in them. You will want to serve her."

Banks had had enough. He made his move on Bill while the old man stood transfixed by the sight of that quivering, spreading wall.

He used his binds as a garrote, wrapping it around the old man's neck. Banks fell backwards and pulled as hard as he could. The two collapsed to the floor. The Henry clattered to the ground. Banks wrenched harder. The old man's feet kicked at the floor.

The wall of flesh jiggled. A great rush of air filled the room and more spores filled the air. Things became soupy and rank.

Silas keened angrily, dove for the Henry, and sent it clattering across the room in his attempt to grab it. No gunslinger, was Silas.

By the time Silas reached the gun, Uncle Bill had ceased his struggling.

"Say goodbye to your uncle, you sick peckerwood fuck–" Banks said but then Silas brought the butt of the rifle down on Banks' face and Banks' tasted blood and swallowed teeth and Silas brought the butt down again upon his head and Banks' thoughts went all to shivering stars and the full black darkness of the deep places of the Earth.

What dreams that came were of Celia, Celia the woman, and her face in the darkness. And he was being carried and it hurt and then the stars wheeled and Celia was gone and Banks was rolling.

Elmore Banks was a bad man. And his gun had a name. And her name was Celia. And Celia was missing. But Banks' knife was still in his boot and that had to count for something. He drew the knife and used it to saw through the rope around his wrist. He crawled out of that ditch and found his feet.

The knife shone dully in the day's fading light. His insides hurt. His tongue felt swollen and too-thick and slushy. Like a wad of bills left out in the rain.

He'd find Silas. He'd do what work he could up close. He'd get his Celia back. Kiss her one last goodbye.

Elmore Banks was a gunslinger. And a bad man. And the toughest motherfucker in these parts.

Fixable

Sheliah Lindsey

THE DOCTOR assured us our baby girl was fixable.

He showed us diagrams, an engineer's careful notations, and told us she could be made whole. That her cloudy left eye could be replaced with an array of lenses and mirrors that could transfer light to the brain, that her spine could be straightened with a metal corset like a cradle around her chest. That he could make an automaton hand to grip the malformed stump of her wrist and connect small wires under her skin called nerves, that he could fix a bellows between her ribs and up her throat to compensate for a thready, undersized left lung.

The doctor told us that it was the factories, or perhaps the smog the coal-burning train engines dumped into the air, or it was something called 'trace elements' now present in our food. It disrupted pregnancies, halted essential processes in the womb. He said that a few decades ago our baby girl would have been dead barely after she was born, leaving us nothing but a tiny grave to dig. But today, by the grace of modern science, she could live a happy, full life, as able as a normal child, although she would never be normal.

The thought did not excite in me the same relief that shone in my husband's eyes. How could science claim to solve a problem of its own creation? But I kept my silence as he signed the papers. Surely a not-quite-human daughter was better than none at all?

His hand clenched mine, white at the knuckles, and we cried together when the doctor set to work, like we had the night she was born.

When he finished, I was the only one who cried. I told them they were tears of joy.

I lied.

She is not the darling girl the neighborhood women have on their hips when I visit. The metal of her frame digs into skin if I try to balance her against my hip, and she is so heavy I would be hard-pressed to lift her with one arm alone. Not that she can often be persuaded to sit. Our six-month-old girl stands unaided on a spine forged from metals strong enough to hold up a building. She walks when other children crawl—no, she *runs,* in wide, tottering strides like a wolf pup after a hare. She breathes in great gasps and can stay underwater what seems like eternity, watching other children play from below the surface of our pond.

My husband dotes on the child—delights in her. They chop firewood together, laughing each time she splits a log twice as big around as her waist in one blow. He calls her Bell because of the sound her bare metal body makes when something rebounds off it. I watch as my husband removes my daughter's hand and he teaches her how to even out the dents, heads bent close, almost touching, their laughter ringing almost as clearly as the hammer on her tin fingers.

I, in turn, sew her pretty dresses and lace gloves. She doesn't like the gloves. She never wears them, preferring the glint of her own hands in the sunlight to the seashell-pale of the gloves. If I force them on her, she rips them off, leaving a puddle of lace scraps at her feet. I have to make her dresses loose, because anything tighter hurts the binding in her spine, or so I think, as she cries whenever I dress her. They are strange tears, dripping from her clockwork eye like water from a ledge, more a product of excess fluid than genuine emotion.

When I tried to teach her the waltz, she squeezed my hand too hard and stepped on my foot until my ankle sprained. The doctor said it was clumsiness due to being six months old and made so much stronger than bone, but I swear there was malice in her eyes, an edge in the turning gears of her clockwork socket.

I say nothing to my husband or the doctor, of course. They are convinced she is an angel on Earth, the first in hundreds, thousands, of children snatched from death by the sneakthief science.

Instead I listen to her heart while my husband sleeps. It keeps time audibly, tick, tick, tick, in time with our clock, except that she does not ring on the hour, although she delights in every chime, and occasionally stands in front of our timepiece, still as a statue, imitating its hourly calls.

She must be rewound at midnight, like the rest of our machines. She can't do it herself yet and so I must wind her up as she sleeps. Sometimes when I twist the key, she will wake and look at me, expressionless, motionless, until she is fully wound and I leave the room.

Her heart is nearly stopped. I should go now.

The One in the Night-Storm Dress

Andrea Martinez Corbin

PETRA ATTENDED her first Death's Ball when she was sixteen. Younger than most by three years, but her parents conceded in the face of Petra's ceaseless arguments: first, she had pledged to Death when she was fourteen, and been accepted without caveat or hesitation; second, no one would know who she was behind the traditional mask, so questions of age were moot; finally, Petra had the perfect outfit: a dress that shimmered indigo-violet, tailored to her boxy torso in a way that made her feel both powerful and delicate, like a knife made of damselfly wings. The skirt twirled and draped and gathered like storm clouds, and the sleeves were made of black lace that faded into the air.

No one could deny that dress.

On the night of her first Ball, Petra slicked her hair like

crow's feathers, pinned jewels like stars against it, donned a dark mask, and prepared to dance her shoes into dust. A butler at the entrance pinned a white rose to her dress before she could stop him, marking her as a new attendee. Before she could tear the rose away, a woman took her arm and ushered her in, voice gentle and constant, like a susurrus of wind in new leaves.

Petra immediately spied Death in the crowd. A shimmering opalescent gown curved over Its shapely frame, and Its mask was white. No one else would be, *could* be in unpainted porcelain. Surrounded by people trying not to look like they surrounded It, Death only looked toward the man asking for a dance. This one night, they entertained Death, and Death would come for no one. Petra always wondered how much truth was in the Ball's founding legend, that long, long ago, a woman had stopped a plague by inviting Death to dance.

The woman still spoke. "And I won't ask your name, of course. Come, let's treat ourselves to the golden punch. Will you wait for an invitation to dance?" The woman turned to look at her, eyes visible behind her painted mask. Her dress was all purples and greens; the ensemble suggested the elegance of the peacock without the haughtiness.

"Do you think it would be long if I waited?" Here, of all places, Petra hoped she might be treated as any other young woman. Not plain Petra, quiet Petra, uninteresting and forgettable Petra.

The woman passed Petra a drink and said, "I don't imagine you'll finish your punch."

To Petra's shock, it was no exaggeration. Behind her mask's smoky swirls of blacks and blues, she barely took a sip before there came a young man wearing a half-mask, hand extended. She took it. The song was short, and at the end, he whispered, "Another?"

"How impolite it would be to the other attendees if we monopolized each other's time," Petra said, the words spilling forth more easily than they ever had before. "If you're very lucky, you may find me for a tango later."

The man laughed low in his throat, pressing his lips to her bare hand. "Until then."

Petra let herself be swept back to the edge of the dance, only to find another man offering his hand to her. And she danced, until her breath was short and a sheen of sweat rose on her skin, until she was dizzy with masks and colors, until she requested, at last, an escort to make sure she made it back to the refreshments. Her partner, a man in a light gold mask, laughed and linked their arms. Soon he placed a full cup in Petra's hand, and led her to a table. Sitting next to her golden-masked dancer, Petra found herself in conversation with a woman in rainbows, a tall man picking at the tie of his plain blue mask, and a man in a suit so dark he nearly matched Petra.

"You can't be serious," the rainbow woman was saying. "He's *flaunting*. Let him settle first."

"Be daring—find him without the mask, later," said Blue Mask. Rainbow laughed. "He's certainly not dedicated to anonymity tonight."

"Who?" Petra asked.

"There's a new pledge of Love flitting around tonight. Must be his first event," Rainbow said. She gestured lazily. A man across the way wore a half-mask so pink it was almost obscene, and bowed his way from person to person, handing out roses that he seemed to draw from nowhere.

The man in the dark suit raised his chin. "I think it's sweet. Not everyone gets accepted by Love, after all."

"Of course not! Love gets nearly as many pledges as Life."

"But Life accepts them all."

"Life isn't choosy," Rainbow said.

"Life is everywhere," Blue Mask said.

"So is Death, and Death accepts only one," Dark Suit countered.

"Can you imagine pledging to Death?" Blue Mask shivered theatrically. "What would Death ask of you?"

Blue Mask was either being silly, or didn't know much about Exemplars at all. Petra said, "None of Them ask anything of Their pledges."

"I heard that Wealth takes your youth."

A mess of voices responded: "That's absurd." "Who said that?" "What would Wealth want with youth?" "Have you known a Wealth's pledge?"

Blue Mask held up his hands in surrender. "It's what I heard."

"Oh, yes, me too. And I heard that Death turns you into a pumpkin and brings back your childhood pet as a skeleton," Petra said. The table turned to look at her. Behind her mask, she bit her lip, eyes wide.

They burst into laughter, and Petra relaxed.

"I heard there was a new one recently! It's been long enough," Rainbow said.

"He didn't even die, that's why it's been so long. Death *took* him,' Blue Mask said. Then, when the table stared at him, dry disbelief nearly audible, he added, "I was at the funeral. The casket was empty."

Rainbow turned to him for a long, silent moment. "You were not. You would've been no more than twelve, and no children were there."

Blue Mask crossed his arms and leaned back. Rainbow did the same, her shoulders drawn back, head cocked in challenge. After a long, tense moment, Blue Mask relaxed, putting a hand nervously up to the tie of his mask again, and said, "Fine. I wasn't."

"And it was no mystery. He died in his sleep, didn't he? Surrounded by family, I heard, everyone there to say goodbye," Petra said wistfully. A long full life, she thought, leaving the world to every person he had loved.

"In his sleep, yes," Rainbow said, though underneath Petra thought she heard someone laugh.

"And he's to be credited for our clean water," Petra said. "My grandfather said he'd never seen the river so clear in the city."

"Yes, yes," Dark Suit said, amusement in his voice. "But we could argue all night whether his pledge had a bit to do with that."

"Of course it did! Your pledge defines you. The Exemplar touches you, your life," Petra said.

"Indeed, my dear," Rainbow said. Petra was mollified, but knew they were humoring her. Not everyone still thought the Exemplars meant much in this modern age. The steam engine would be a finer Exemplar to them than Death or Love. Pledging had never been universal, but there was a time when it had been more common, Petra had been told. When these things mattered, when many carried their mark, their token, their pledge to Life or Hearth or Plenty.

Petra looked across the room and searched for a white mask.

"Who's the new pledge to Death, then?" Dark Suit asked.

"They haven't presented themselves," Blue Mask said, with audible disappointment.

"That's not unusual for Death's, is it?" said Petra's dance partner.

"It gives us time for sport," Dark Suit said. "Have you been to the butcher's on Fleet?"

"Oh! That butcher boy, the one with the flop of red hair?"

"Him, don't you think?"

Petra reveled in their wild guesses, animated and eager and utterly wrong on every count. They never came close to guessing her. For the sheer fun of playing along, Petra suggested a woman she'd taken piano lessons from, citing the smell of death in her home as proof. The smell was a cleaning solvent, dust, and flowers past their prime, but laying out the facts lacked the thrill of assigning her falsely to Death.

"Friend, look out!" Blue Mask interrupted the guessing, flinging his hand toward the dance floor. "Your amour is getting away from you."

The new pledge of Love was dancing extremely closely with a woman. Petra could see Dark Suit's shoulders straighten with the challenge.

"Best hurry," Rainbow said, more generously than Blue Mask's melodramatic teasing.

"You don't honestly think he'll fall for you, for all time and eternity?" Blue Mask scoffed.

"Even children know that's not true," Petra said, trying to be as generous with her tone as Rainbow. But she blushed under her mask, thinking of what she *had* heard about Love's pledges. Hushed rumors about the time of your life, even if it was only one night.

"I'm no fool. But I've never been with a pledge of Love, and I, for one, want first-hand knowledge," Dark Suit said, fingers stroking the knot of his tie with exquisite slowness. His attention was halfway across the room long before he bothered to stand up.

"Wait for me!" Rainbow rose, revealing a skirt of layers and layers of chiffon, moving like clouds of the wildest sunset. "I want to steal his dance partner."

A moment after the others left, Blue Mask asked Petra for a dance. She looked at him, fidgeting and overdramatic and a little too mocking of sincerity, and declined in favor of refilling her cup. It wouldn't be long, after all. By the refreshments, she shifted her weight, making her skirt swish and swirl. Thank the Exemplars for her dance lessons. Thank the Exemplars for her mask, and the voice she had found behind it.

Paused at the other end of the refreshments table, Death watched the crowd. Petra tried to hold herself as still and regal as Death. She wondered if it were entirely true, that Exemplars asked nothing, as her drink's chill shivered into her fingers. Hearth was her father's pledge, and they seemed to be a family like any other, no difference in their home or meals or anything else. Petra's mother had never pledged. The Exemplars unsettled her, and she couldn't bear to be near such strange, inhuman things. Inhuman, Petra thought, with a smile. How inhuman could one be at a ball?

As she lay in bed after the Ball, exhausted and sleepless, images of rainbows and white masks flitting through her head, Petra had a moment of revelation. She would save her dress. A little gift. The most beautiful thing in her life, she would keep for Death and wear again at Its Ball, transforming herself each year in honor of her pledge.

———•—•—•———

The custom among attendees of Death's Ball was to spend months with tailors and dressmakers, creating new looks each year. At Petra's second Ball, when the whispers hissed around her, Petra was not surprised. Judgment. Confusion. Curiosity. A copycat? Or the same attendee, faced with the misery of being unable to afford new fashions? Petra's patience settled in her bones and she danced, admiring Death, dresses, top hats, and all.

Her third year, a few attendees realized it was the same

woman, three years in a row. The One in the Night-Storm Dress. The murmur spread as the crowd circled the shining dance floor.

At Petra's fourth, fifth, sixth Balls, the whispers grew admiring, even jealous. It hadn't been her intention, the acclaim. Only a pledge's honor to her Exemplar. But to say she minded the flutters of praise would be a dreadful lie—the rest of the year Petra was a footnote, an average citizen of average means and perhaps below-average looks. At Death's Ball, she was a legend. In the Night-Storm Dress she was charming and a flirt, which only made them clamor more. She was a princess, they said; no, a duchess on the lam; or better yet, a pauper in a stolen dress.

Soon, Petra thought. When the time was right, she'd tell them she was the pledge. When she had done something a tenth as grand as clean water, or when she could give a reason that didn't sound childish. She'd known she was childish even as she pledged years before, but that made the pledge no less serious. Protecting her family was utterly serious. There had been no one protecting them thus far. Petra grew up watching six different anniversaries her mother quietly kept. Looking at a baby's bonnet that had never been worn; visiting a small grave early in the morning; or meticulously cleaning the framed photo of herself and Petra's father with a two young boys, taken before Petra was born. Petra had no siblings. She remembered one, faintly, or at least she remembered being prepared for an infant to arrive, but nothing of the infant herself.

Petra would tell them, when she had something to say.

Petra went to the Ball each year and danced.

Despite the story that grew around her in those years, one persistent tale was probably untrue—that she danced with Death, perhaps all the way into her bed. Whoever started that rumor was inventive at best, malicious at worst.

No, Petra never once asked Death to dance.

———————

On the night of her tenth Death's Ball, Petra entered with her dress as darkly gleaming as the day it was made. As she passed her cloak to a butler at the door, she smiled under her mask. At last, at last, the night of the Ball, making her heart sing. At last, her dress and her mask. At last she was nameless and perfect.

Petra never responded to the rumors, but that meant she never denied them, curating her allure. It was wonderful, for a night, having her pick of dance partners. Being wanted, blatantly. For as long as a dance, she was royalty in hiding to this person, a trickster to that, more of a mystery than anyone else in their masks.

At the end of her first dance Petra bowed to her partner. When she rose, her eyes rested on Death. It wore a dress that was like dawn to Petra's night, pale yellows and rose fading to soft green like dewy grass. It stood smaller than usual, as though younger, looking more like Petra had when she'd pledged than It looked like any of the other attendees at the Ball. A mirror. Dawn and night, calm and storm, the certainty of youth. Petra blinked at Death, and felt spoken to.

She waited two more dances, rested for one, and looked out on the room. The height of attendance, when most everyone had arrived and hardly anyone had left.

Petra swept toward the raised stage where the musicians were, and caught the first violin before he started another song. After a moment of silent gesturing, he stood and helped her onto the stage. At the lack of music, a murmur crept through the crowd, and they slowly turned to find Petra, waiting.

Through the eye holes in her mask, everyone glittered,

and Death stood out, like always.

"My dears! My friends, my loves, my fellow celebrants! For years, you have wondered who I am. I know the stories. I started a few," Petra said, cocking her hip. The crowd laughed. "Tonight, after ten years, I thought you deserved to know why I wear this dress—aside from the fact that it's irresistible. I don't know the last time I lacked for a dance partner."

Petra blew a kiss at the crowd, angled like it was for a particular favorite. Her eyes moved from person to person and always darted back to Death. It *had* given her a sign, hadn't It? Underneath that mask, Its expression must be urging her on. But she couldn't tell if It even looked at her, or laughed.

She had gone too far to doubt herself, and doubting was for Petra, not the One in the Night-Storm Dress. So she said, "I wear this dress each year like a sacred uniform because this Ball is sacred to me. This Ball... is a celebration of *my* Exemplar."

Someone screamed in the crowd—shock, vindication, Petra couldn't tell. The room burst into chatter, and Petra took a deep, long breath of it. All this, for her. For Death and her, she thought.

Petra stepped toward the edge of the raised stage and two people near the front hurried forward, hands at the ready to help her step down. It felt like dancing, floating down the scant distance to land lightly. Their hands lingered, and others reached out, with shouted invitations, but Petra kept moving. The crowd shifted with her, like her breath was music guiding a new dance, one with the sole purpose of bringing Petra to stand in front of Death.

She had wanted to prove herself first, but perhaps she had gotten things all inverted. Mirrored and distorted. It wasn't night and secrets, but still the dawn of her time as a pledge. Petra faced Death in silence, the entire Ball watching. It was childish to think she could hide and burst out, fully formed and accomplished. They had to grow together.

Petra held her hand out, palm up. Behind her mask, she opened her mouth for a breath of air, a short inhale before speaking—

The doors burst open. A man stood framed by the darkness outside, and cold night air gusted in, carrying the smell of snow. The man tore off his mask to reveal his pale face. "Death," he said, and everyone looked to Petra and Death, but the man wasn't done. "There's been a death."

The commotion that rose around Petra and Death was greater than the one caused by her announcement, as some people scrambled toward the doors and some backed away, as though they could escape the man's words. It couldn't be, she thought, echoing words that were flying around the room. Her hand was still raised in invitation when the man was able to shout over the noise again, calling Petra's name. Her hand shook. He was searching for the pledge of Death, surely, for some unknowable reason, to demand her presence, her explanation, insist that as Death's pledge she would be able to explain all this, but she couldn't move to acknowledge him until Death walked into the crowd, leaving Petra alone.

When she faced the panicked butler, Petra identified herself and clasped his shaking hands. "What can I do?"

"Oh, oh, my dear girl," the man said. "Nothing. I'm so sorry. Your parents' carriage overturned—"

Petra's ears rang; the rest of the sentence faded. As he spoke, Petra spun around. He grabbed her arm, but she wasn't fleeing, she was looking—until she found It, spotted It yards away in the crowd, implacable in Its mask, the same as all night, the same as always. Petra said nothing more that night, and for days after in her empty house.

———•—•—•———

The night was crisp, winter late to arrive, when the Ball came again. As soon as she was safely ensconced in her carriage, Petra leaned leaned back heavily and closed her eyes, focusing on the weight of the porcelain against her face as her carriage wheeled noisily over a long cobblestone drive. When it creaked to a stop, she exited quickly. Music already poured out of the building. Petra paused at the entry to take a breath and gather herself, straighten her spine, tug at her gloves.

The Ball was grander than ever. The hall gleamed; a larger band played, now with a singer; a short list of scheduled performances greeted Petra at the door—all of it meant to make up for the year before. More gold, more glamour, more everything for Death!

More everything—! Except the One in the Night-Storm Dress. The governor himself had visited Petra and asked that she not return. Or, for Exemplars' sakes, only come in true anonymity. Everyone knew the Night-Storm Dress was the pledge of Death, that the pledge was Petra, that Petra had always worn the Night-Storm Dress. After the spectacle she had made last year and the turmoil and uncertainty of the last twelve months, Petra was more aware of the crowd than ever. She forced herself to take slow, even steps.

She had chosen a purple dress that shimmered with blue in certain lights, which fit her well but not so well as she'd like; it complemented both her dark mask and her pale violet gloves. The gloves were tight. They had been her mother's, and the stiff fingers would make little difference in dancing. Though there was no logical reason for Petra not to dress as she liked, she had yielded in terms of the dress. But to give up her mask would be to give up herself entirely, and it was one loss beyond what she could bear. She tugged her glove and strode toward refreshments, as though this were a year like any other.

"You have some nerve."

With an exhale, Petra turned. A man in a silky vermillion suit stitched with intricate black designs stared at her, and from the tightness in his voice, she imagined his face was red as well.

"I was only serving myself some punch," Petra said. If she hadn't yet found her charm again—perhaps it *was* in the dress, after all—then she could be stubbornly obtuse until everyone gave up.

The man snatched the empty glass from her hand and said, "You'll ruin everything *again.* Do you want It to take more of us?"

"I don't know what you mean," Petra said, reaching for another glass.

"I remember that damned mask," he said. An audience was gathering, trying not to look like it gathered. Half-glances turning into full, a gap like a stage between the crowd and the pair of them. "Everyone remembers that mask. What were you thinking, wearing it again? That the Exemplar would overlook it? Your arrogant narcissism for the past decade was bound to upset the balance we had with the Exemplar, even without your haughty display last year."

"Pardon?" Petra said, through her teeth. Tension ran through her muscles and nausea rose in her stomach. With great care, she set down the empty glass and turned to fully face the man as he ranted.

"Your ridiculous speech is the reason the Exemplar took them. You are aware of that, aren't you? You disrupted the Ball, put yourself at the center where only Exemplars belong, and you disrespected—no, you insulted the Exemplar—"

"You can say Its name! My goodness, are you a child? Death. Say it." Petra paused, but the man snapped his mouth shut. She shook her head. "Do you know anything about Exemplars, or do you just enjoy scolding people without full knowledge of anything in this world? My good sir, if you do insist on berating me, let us at least be on equal ground. Our entire audience knows who I am—but who are you?"

The man clenched his fist by his side and was silent.

"It doesn't matter!" A woman in the crowd, though Petra couldn't tell who. "He's right. You ruined the purpose of the Ball and Death punished you!"

"Do you think the governor would allow the Ball to continue if it were so easily ruined? If that were its fragile purpose?" Petra turned so she spoke to all, not just the man who had confronted her. "The purpose of this Ball is not to trick Death into revelry in order to prevent Its work. How could it? Death Itself doesn't cause the cessation of life any more than Life causes two people to create a third."

"But there never was a death during a Ball before," another woman called out.

"Wasn't there? How far back did we take note? And how many times was there a death early the next morning? How many times did someone choose to say nothing until dawn? Even if there had truly been no deaths, it would mean nothing. Only that we had all fooled ourselves into seeing fate where only coincidence lives," Petra said. A moment of silence, only the band playing on, and Petra exhaled, looked down at her gloves—her mother's gloves—and repeated, "All of us, fooled."

"You think you know Death?" the second woman asked. She'd come to the front of the crowd, short and stout and beautiful in a dress like a sparrow. Her voice was not harsh, only curious. If she was the only one in the crowd not blaming Petra, that was enough. Petra focused on her.

"I know that Death was here when my parents died. And I believe that Death was there, too, at the carriage accident. If Death could only be one place at once, what a poor Exemplar It would be," Petra said. "Death comes when the breath leaves the body, but Death does not steal that air."

"I'm sure we're all reassured, hearing that from the pledge who Death punished," the man said.

"Exemplars do not—" Petra started to make the same points again, but the crowd was breaking up.

"You don't know a thing," the man in vermillion said. "You'd be better off renouncing your pledge."

"She just needs time to learn better," said the sparrow-dress woman, turning away. "She clearly hasn't even considered that it's likely an actor under that white mask each year."

"Actors would talk!" Petra called out, but the woman waved her hand, like she was scattering Petra's words into the air.

For the next hour, no one approached to ask her to dance, but she was certain they spoke about her. As she waited, Petra seemed to merit hardly even a glance, and the anxiety that her dress used to banish bubbled up in her chest, filling her lungs. It had been foolish to return, foolish to wear the mask, foolish to argue. She should have stayed home as the governor asked. Petra sipped pale champagne punch through a straw under her mask, grateful for the placidity of the porcelain.

Petra stared down at her gloves. A pressure like a stone weighed on her chest, crushing breath from her lungs. It was impossible to ask for a dance. Too much time had passed. Whenever she gathered the courage to abandon the Ball, she would return to a silent, empty home, her shoes unscuffed by clumsy partners, her gown as pressed and clean as when she donned it. Perhaps it was better to be Death's pledge alone in the house of the dead. Perhaps the man was right and she had ruined it; or woman was right, and it was an actor every year, play-acting in Death's place. Or both, both the actor mocking her beliefs and Death knowing her disrespect. Ah, best to give up and go home—

A hand extended before Petra, gloved in white. A crisp sleeve, and cufflinks with shining mother-of-pearl inlay. Petra looked up to see a white mask. Death wore a dress suit; sleek jacket with tails over the white vest and shirt, all fitted ambiguously and perfectly. Death was ever Death, yet had changing form; this year It was not male, not female, but a vision nonetheless in white tie.

This was her moment. Petra took Death's hand. The music seemed to take a breath, every instrument skipping a note as Petra rose.

For an eternity and a heartbeat, they stood posed, not moving to the dance floor; Petra's hand rested in Death's and they gazed at each other, one placid mask to the other. Young and naive, Petra had chosen Death for her loyalty, with a secret hope in her heart, now fractured. At each Ball, Petra waited, never once approaching the object of her loyalty, watching while every attendee asked It for a dance; that was the order of things. For one night, Death waited for an invitation.

And then Death came to Petra.

She gripped Its hand with a sudden ferocity, feeling bones under skin, Its fingers contorting, but Death didn't try to pull away so Petra drew It toward her. Petra knew her chest and neck were flushed, could feel the heat of her skin.

"You couldn't have waited until morning?" she hissed. Death moved Its arm and drew Petra closer, inexorably into Its arms. "For me?" she said, voice drier than her eyes, which stung. "A few hours, that's all. Then it would have nothing to do with this night. Nothing to do—separate from—from you—"

On the dance floor, couples parted to allow them to glide wherever Death wished. Petra had never been so close to Death. It was as warm and graceful as any dance partner. When her parents died, she had been making a fool of herself while Death stayed at arm's length.

"Did they see you? Were you there?" she asked.

As the song ended, Death continued to lead Petra, and the band took up a melody from their steps.

"Are you even real?" she whispered.

Petra stared up at the white mask. There were no eyeholes. The music sounded raucous to her ears, too loud for her thoughts. Her mask captured her breath and held it close, foggy and stifling, making her want to rip it off for the first time in her life.

Instead, she lifted her hand from Death's shoulder—in that moment blood singing with a new desire that beat from her broken heart, thrumming with the petty need to unmask a monster for all to see, burning with a grief that would never leave her; she was dizzy with anticipation of a new roar from the crowd, whether they would look to her as the one who finally showed Death for what It really was, or as the pledge who kept destroying the Ball out of selfishness; her head spun like she'd stopped drawing breath, but she was braced upright in Death's arms—and Petra reached for Its mask.

As her fingers grasped toward the ribbon, they fought against the tight fabric of her gloves, and she hesitated.

Strange, inhuman things.

What mortal nonsense all of this was, the shame and vanity, the idea of revenge, the glamour and the shine. Petra's skin prickled. The suit could be empty, for all it mattered to the Ball or her pledge. Her arm ached from hovering above Death's shoulder, and in the corner of her eye she saw how still the dancers were, how those who moved were out of time with the music, with so much focus once again on Petra and Death.

Petra untied the ribbon of her mask and tossed it to the floor, where it cracked in two. She lost track of it as Death swept her away in a waltz.

Kaffeklatsch with
Madeleine Swann
and Andrew McCurdy

Andrew: Madeleine, welcome to the Café of Curiosities, where we sip from our favourite libation and chat with authors. Thank you for agreeing to sit down to join me for this issue.

Madeleine: No problem, excited to talk to you!

Andrew: Your story, "All She Needs," has a fascinating and rather unique character, in Little Miss Emily. Alluring and repulsive and ultimately very sympathetic. Who I really want to learn about is the housekeeper. Tell me more about Gladys.

Madeleine: Gladys thinks she knows what's best for Emily, but it's a sick and stifling love. She'd never see that though, she's very firmly set in her ways. She'll do whatever she can to reach the outcome she feels is the right one.

Andrew: When you are writing a story, such as "All She Needs," how do you know when it is done, no more tinkering, time to send it off?

Madeleine: To be honest I was still tinkering just before I sent it to you. It's a difficult one, each time you read through there'll always be something you want to change. It's probably a gut feeling about whether it says what you want clearly enough.

Andrew: I have a copy of your book *Fortune Box* on my iPad. I'm looking forward to reading it. Could you tell our readers a little something about it—and, do you have a favourite parcel among them?

Madeleine: I hope you like it! *Fortune Box* is an interconnected collection of short stories about a mysterious company, Tower Ltd, who send packages to random people throughout The City. Each package could be just what they need—or an absolute nightmare.
    My personal favourite probably isn't one of the 'best' ones—most seem to like the first story of the bad date or the man who finds himself hated online—but the second story with the girls at college is based largely on my own experiences, minus the gore and fantastic elements of course. It's near to my heart because I hope one day my friend Susie reads it.

Andrew: As I was planning for this interview, I had the site MADELEINESWANN.WORDPRESS.COM open on my laptop when my eleven-year-old joined me. Normally she doesn't give my work a second glance but you caught her eye. Tell me something about your fantastic sense of style.

Madeleine: Kids love to look at me, it's really cool. I love the 60s and the 20s, so I formed a style I call 'psychedelic flapper,' where my clothes are 1920s with a psychedelic twist. By the way, my main website is madeleineswann.com, I don't really blog anymore since I started talking with my mouth online.

Andrew: What are you working on now?

Madeleine: I'm working on another novella with the help of Christoph Paul from Clash Books, who's assisting with the structure. It's a crime set in an alternative 1920s New York overgrown with strange alien vegetation. I'm also editing a children's book and starting on some short stories.

Andrew: What do you like best about your own writing and what impression would you like people to get from your work?

Madeleine: Nicholas Day from Strangehouse Books once described my work as malicious whimsy and I think that might be perfect. I want to give my perspective on the world and people in society who are often ignored, in a way that allows my imagination to ooze from my brain cells.

Andrew: How often do you read for pleasure, and what do you look for when you read the works of other authors? Conversely, what are some of your pet peeves about works you have not enjoyed?

Madeleine: I read a lot and enjoy a wide variety of things from biographies to surrealism to horror, history, comedy and bizarro. I love something that makes my imagination crackle. I've tried to get into straight literary fiction and there are some that I love, but generally, it just doesn't excite me. I'm sure they make lots of wonderful and well-observed commentary about the world but it always leaves me feeling flat.

Andrew: It is interesting that you mention bizarro, I was chatting with a friend recently about this genre. How would you define bizarro, and are there any particular stories or authors in this category you are comfortable recommending?

Madeleine: Bizarro to me is an umbrella term for modern weird, so it can be anything from disturbing to weird horror to absurdist to surreal and more. I'm very influenced by Russian absurdists, Haruki Murakami, The Mighty Boosh, Leonora Carrington, Julia Davis, Robert Aickman and Junji Ito, so make of that what you will.

Personally, I'm a big fan of Gabino Iglesias, Autumn Christian, Leza Cantoral, Kevin Donihe, MP Johnson, WD Frank, Julia Platz-Halter, Mame Diene and Matthew Revert (not an exhaustive list by any means), they're all quite different but are all my cup of tea in various ways.

Myself and the other British Bizarros have formed the British Bizarro Community (BBC), an informal group who help each other out, go to cons together and will be releasing a charity anthology this year.

Andrew: What is your favourite line from your own writing—published or not?

Madeleine: I love this section from "Invite Ghosts And Earn Pounds," read on *The Wicked Library* podcast:

> The fluorescent figure of a man with a long beard and sunken eyes looms from the wall. He stares into nothing and his voice is droning on and on and I think I recognise it… "Perhaps the lady is a natural beauty, or perhaps she's using Sparkle Cutie." Over and over again it sings the jingle until I yell at it to shut up. It ignores me.
>
> "Hmm…wha?" Mike opens his eyes and looks up at me.

"What is that thing doing?"

Mike rolls over and tells me to go back to sleep but I shake him awake. "I knew you'd get like this. We get extra money from advertisers if one of the spirits sings their jingle for five minutes. Just ignore it."

Andrew: What do you value the most in feedback and reviews from your readers?

Madeleine: I think it's valuable to hear from people whether you're on the right track culturally. I'd hate to be one of those writers who unthinkingly uses an insensitive trope and refuses to learn from it. Also, just general feedback is always important.

Andrew: Finally, what do you enjoy most about being a writer?

Madeleine: The fact that I can work in my pyjamas, that I can lose myself in a world that feels so real, and also that I've barely even begun.

Andrew: Cheers to working in pyjamas and cheers to you,

Madeleine. Thank you for joining me for this edition of the Kaffeeklatsch.

Madeleine: Thanks for having me, and hopefully you'll join me on Twitter where you'll be treated to numerous hideous face pictures.

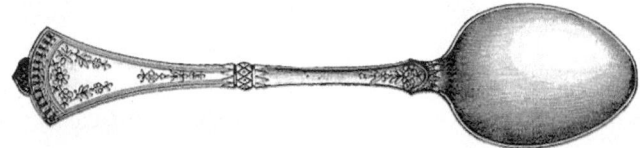

Take Five

Samantha Lee

ZOOT SHOOK HIS HEAD but the fuzziness remained. If it hadn't been so uncool, he might have even asked 'Where am I?' His last memory was of blowing the ultimate note in *Satin Doll*... then came the blackout.

And yet, here he was, sitting in this very plush dive (a dive wherein, he was sure, he had never before set foot) with a drink in one hand, a cheroot in the other and a tingling anticipation such as he hadn't felt since he was a kid in downtown Chicago.

"Hey man."

Zoot looked up in surprise. A tall dark stranger stood observing him nonchalantly. What could only have been described as a sardonic smile was plastered across his kisser.

"Hey," said Zoot, taking the new dude in. No doubt about it, the cat was sharp... as a tack. The creases in the trousers of his pinstripe suit would have done justice to a razor and the points of his narrow lapels could easily have doubled as toothpicks. The blood-red carnation in his buttonhole was the only spot of color in the entire tasteful collage. He was wearing a black silk shirt, a white satin tie, and a dove-grey fedora. His feet were hidden by the table-cloth, but Zoot would have wagered his sax to a penny whistle that the man was wearing spats. He was that kind of a dude.

"May I?" asked the stranger, and before Zoot could say 'yea' or 'nay' he had eased his elegant frame into an adjoining gilt chair. "Drink?" he enquired politely, and Zoot said he didn't mind if he did.

The stranger pointed a perfectly manicured fingernail at Zoot's near-empty glass and before his astonished eyes, the level of the corn-coloured liquid rose until it was lapping the brim.

"Now listen, man..." Zoot began, but his companion casually raised a silencing hand.

"Show's about to start," he said.

A hush fell over the crowded salon as the red velvet curtains swished back to reveal a big-band dressed in scarlet and black. Pink spotlights ricocheted off their glinting instruments and threw dancing flames onto the dark orange backcloth.

Zoot's eyes began to pop as they travelled over the brass section. This surely was some line-up. In fact, the entire band consisted of the grooviest selection of heads ever collected under one roof. And yet something niggled at the back of his mind.

It wasn't until a very famous black lady singer stepped up to the microphone to inquire of the assembled throng '*Am I blue?*' that the penny dropped. That particular lady singer was also very dead. As were the rest of the ensemble.

Zoot closed his eyes and abandoned himself to the sound. It was like nothing he'd ever heard before. The music lapped around his eardrums like liquid silk.

"I made it," he whispered to himself. "Man, I actually made it. I never had myself figured for heaven... but here I am."

"Why don't you sit in?" suggested a smooth voice at his elbow.

Zoot shook himself out of his euphoria and found himself staring into the dark stranger's mesmeric yellow eyes.

"What me?" he gasped in awe. "Me? Play with those cats? You gotta be joking."

The tall dark stranger said far from it, he owned the joint and Zoot only had to say the word and he could be up there with his peers.

To Zoot's objection that he hadn't brought his sax, he responded by producing one out of thin air. A gleaming, gold object, the like of which Zoot had never been able to afford in all his drink-sodden life. He hefted the instrument lovingly in his hands, put the reed to his mouth and blew a few practice arpeggios.

It was as though the sax played him. Its rich, fluid tones fired Zoot's long-dormant ambition and soothed any butterflies he might have felt about playing with the illustrious gathering of musicians on stage.

"Why not?" he chortled. "What've I gotta loose?"

The trumpet player waved a welcoming hand in greeting as he clambered up the rostrum steps. The band were into an up-tempo version of Zoot's all-time favorite tune—*Honeysuckle Rose.*

He joined in, playing like he'd never played before, blowing the skids from under every other sax-man there. He even took a solo, one of such brilliance that it elicited an ecstatic response from the packed audience. As one, they got to their collective feet and gave him his first ever standing ovation.

Zoot was beside himself.

The tune wound on and on, until the band had exhausted every nuance of every note, every slight and subtle variation on every theme. And then they went back and started all over again from the top.

Zoot began to flag a little. The old ticker wasn't all that it might have been. He felt that tell-tale twinge in the chest, the numbing sensation in the left arm that heralded an attack. He shuffled across to the band-leader and hissed in his ear.

"Hey man... when do we take a break?"

The trumpet player rolled his eyes in Zoot's direction. They held a hollow emptiness that made his blood run cold. For the first time since Zoot had come up onto the podium, the trumpet player lowered his mouthpiece.

Blood oozed from the splits in an upper lip that was covered in half-healed sores.

"What break?" he said.

And suddenly, Zoot realised that he wasn't in Heaven after all...

Contributors

During the day, author **Beston Barnett** designs and builds furniture in San Diego. At night, he plays Romani jazz. The rest of the time he spends writing quirky stories in which he struggles—never successfully—to leave his characters happily ever after.

Gary Buller is an author from Manchester England where he lives with his partner Lisa and daughters Holly and Evie. He grew up in the Peak District where the hauntingly beautiful landscapes inspired him to write. He is a huge fan of all things macabre, and loves a tale with a twist. He is a member of the Horror Writers Association.

Andrea Martinez Corbin is an author and the founder of the Speculative Boston reading series. Her stories have appeared in *Shimmer, Flash Fiction Online, Podcastle,* and more. Her interactive fiction has appeared in *Sub-Q,* and more projects are available on her website, www.amcorbin.com. On Twitter, she is @rosencrantz.

Santiago Eximeno is a Spanish genre writer who has published several novellas and collections, mainly horror literature and flash fiction. His work has been translated to English, Japanese, French or Bulgarian. You can find him at www.eximeno.com or @santiagoeximeno on Twitter.

Kevin Frost is a shellback who headed inland after developing a mortal terror of Davy Jones. He can often be found managing the *Curiosities* inbox while eating breakfast burritos (smothered, Christmas) at a lonely crossroads diner, and has only occasional bouts of vertigo from living so far from the coast.

Maria Haskins is a Swedish-Canadian writer and translator. She writes speculative fiction and poetry, and currently lives just outside Vancouver with a husband, two kids, and a very large black dog. Her work has appeared in *Flash Fiction Online, Shimmer, Cast of Wonders,* and elsewhere. Find out more on her website, mariahaskins.com, or follow her on Twitter, @mariahaskins.

Toe Keen–an artist currently residing in Spain. Lover of wine, women and song, and right now is smashing up canvas, melting crayons and annihilating brushes as he preps a big-ass graphic novel. Visit his galleries at www.atoekeneffort.weebly.com.

Samantha Lee began writing while she was still a professional performer. Her output is as diverse as it is prolific, covering both fact and fiction and including novels in the sci-fi and dark fantasy genres, self-development and exercise books, short stories and articles, TV series and movie screenplays, literary criticism and poetry. Her work has been translated into French, Dutch, Spanish, Swedish, Italian, German, Croatian, Greek and Chinese.

Sheliah Lindsey was neither born nor raised under a rock, but does claim she was as an excuse for how behind she is on popular culture. She currently resides in Texas, still not under a rock despite her continued insistence to the contrary, where she divides her time unevenly between reading, writing, and Brazilian Jiu Jitsu.

George Edwards Murray is a writer from Maine who currently resides in the heart of steel country. His fiction has appeared, or is forthcoming, in *Daily Science Fiction, Bourbon Penn,* and other venues for strange and troubling stories. Find out more at www.elegantapocalypse.com.

Andrew McCurdy is a writer and editor whose day job as a Speech-Language Pathologist involves helping nonverbal, special needs children access technology to maximize their ability to communicate. He lives in rural Nova Scotia with an eleven-year-old girl, two cats, and a brazen little hamster named *Mouse*–who frequently (and magically) escapes the confines of her cage to taunt the two ancient cats with daring midnight runs across the kitchen floor.

Irene Punti lives in Badalona (Catalonia) with her partner. Before that, she lived for a decade in Tarragona, the former capital of a Roman province and the city which inspired the story that appears in this volume. Irene's stories have appeared in *Gaslandia: a Dieselpunk Anthology* and the *NonBinary Review,* among others.

Alex Stanmyer lives outside of Boston with his archaeologist wife. At night, he writes stories featuring healthy doses of weirdness. By day, he lives the weirdness as a middle school English teacher. His fiction has previously appeared in *Daily Science Fiction.* You can find him on Twitter @StannyLeroy.

Madeleine Swann's novella/short story collection, *Fortune Box,* was published by Eraserhead Press, her second by Strangehouse Books and her first was part of the *New Bizarro Author Series.*

Phil Witte's cartoons have appeared in dozens of publications in the US. and UK, including *The Wall Street Journal, Barron's, Reader's Digest, New Statesman,* and *Private Eye,* as well as in books and greeting cards. His humor books on turning 50 and turning 60 have sold over 150,000 copies.

What is missing from this page? You! Your comics,
your advertisements for fake products, your
curious sketches. We want to fill the back section
with the sort of ephemera that will end each issue
wtih a smile.

To learn more about our submission policies, buy
additional copies, or to find out where you can
listen to audio versions of these stories for free,
visit us on the web at **GalleryCurious.com**, or
send inquiries to CuriousGallery@gmail.com.

Tudor Perpendicular
might not have been
a wise font choice for
setting a title as long
as Mr. Stanmyer sent.

www.ingramcontent.com/pod-product-compliance
Lightning Source LLC
Chambersburg PA
CBHW022021170626
46808CB00003B/1014